THE
SUMMONER'S SINS

Sandal Castle Medieval Thrillers

Book Two

Keith Moray

SAPERE
BOOKS

THE
SUMMONER'S SINS

Published by Sapere Books.

20 Windermere Drive, Leeds, England, LS17 7UZ,
United Kingdom

saperebooks.com

ISBN: 978-1-80055-241-8

Keith Moray is represented by Isabel Atherton at Creative
Authors.

In memory of the Rev Leslie Kitchen, my late father-in-law.
A good and humble priest and an able and knowledgeable historian.

There was a Summoner with us at that Inn,
His face was on fire, like a cherubin,
For he had carbuncles. His eyes were narrow,
He was as hot and lecherous as a sparrow.
Black scabby brows he had, and a thin beard.

Garlic he loved, and onions too, and leeks,
And drinking strong red wine till all was hazy.
Then he would shout and jabber as if crazy,
And wouldn't speak a word except Latin
When he was drunk, such tags as he was pat in:
He only had a few, say two or three,
That he had mugged up out of some decree
No wonder, for he heard them every day.
As you know, a man can teach a jay to call out better than the Pope.
But had you tried to test his wits and grope
For more, you'd have found nothing in his bag.
Then 'Questio quid juris' *was his tag.*

The Summoner's Portrait, *The Canterbury Tales*
Geoffrey Chaucer (1343–1400)

This Summoner in his stirrups stood high;
Upon this Friar his heart was so enraged
That like an aspen leaf he quaked for ire.
"Gentlemen," said he, "but one thing I desire;
I you beseech that, of your courtesy,
Since you have heard this false Friar lie,
Now grant me that me I may tell my tale.
This Friar boasts that he knows hell,
And God knows it, that it is little wonder;
Friars and fiends are but little different."

The Summoner's Prologue, *The Canterbury Tales*

PROLOGUE

Carlisle, 3rd March, 1323

It had been almost one year since Thomas, Earl of Lancaster had been beheaded on the Monk's Hill, a rise in front of Pontefract Castle on St Cuthbert's Day.

Andrew Harclay, at that time Warden of Carlisle, had been there on that dismal day as the snows cleared, leaving tracks of grey slush to match the sombre, leaden sky above, and he had witnessed the barbaric spectacle, beginning with the humiliation of the King's own cousin in front of the braying crowd of commoners. As the army general responsible for capturing Lancaster at the Battle of Boroughbridge, he had been granted the privilege of watching the execution along with His Majesty, King Edward and his noble peers, the Earls of Surrey and Arundel and their Lords the Despensers, from one of the turrets of the castle keep.

He had felt pangs of guilt as he watched the earl, dressed only in a horsehair shirt, much besmeared by snowballs, clods of mud and handfuls of horse dung that had been thrown at him as he was led astride an ass to his execution ground, a priest's hat contemptuously draped upon his head. There, upon the King's orders he was prevented from addressing the crowd. He was gagged by the leather-hooded headsman and thrust down upon the block to face the north, towards Scotland where he had sought help from Robert the Bruce. It was only because he was the King's cousin and therefore carried royal blood in his veins that he had been spared the sentence for treason by being hanged, drawn and quartered.

Harclay remembered feeling sick and shivering almost uncontrollably as the headsman's axe rose quickly and fell to hack the earl's head from his body in one horrific instant. Blood gushed from the severed vessels in the neck stump, covering the block and the ground around it as the body convulsed for some seconds. Yet it was not just the sight that affected him, but the earl's curse that he knew from that moment could never be retracted.

Lancaster himself had knighted Harclay back in 1303, a fact he had used when trying to persuade him to join his rebellion against the King at Boroughbridge, both during the parlay before the battle and again after it, when he had been forced to surrender in the face of Harclay's superior force. And then when conveyed to the dungeons in Pontefract Castle, he had cursed him within hearing of jailors, soldiers and a priest.

'You knave! You traitor! I curse you to eternity and the fires of hell. You, miserable dog, Andrew Harclay will die a traitor's death within one year, as the Lord is my witness.'

But as a reward for winning the battle and bringing Lancaster to his end, King Edward II had made Sir Andrew Harclay the Earl of Carlisle. As a commoner who had become a knight and had then been elevated to the nobility and given the task of guarding his section of the Scottish borders above Carlisle, it seemed his star could not fail to rise. However, his good fortune had come to an end as frustration over Edward's inactivity had grown, and John, the Earl of Brittany's army had been routed by the Scots at the Battle of Old Byland in Yorkshire. John had been taken prisoner, and King Edward himself had only escaped by the skin of his teeth. Harclay had begun negotiating with Robert the Bruce — the leader of the Scottish army — resulting in a treaty in January of that year.

He had done it in good faith and achieved a great result. But his sovereign had not seen it that way.

High treason, the furious King Edward had proclaimed. And it was betrayal by his so-called friend Sir Anthony Lucy that had led to Harclay's arrest in his own castle in Carlisle and a taste of his own dungeon.

He had vomited and felt his bowels threaten to squirt as he was gagged and arraigned in front of Sir Geoffrey le Scrope — Chief Justice of the King's Bench — in his own great hall. Scrope was the very same justice who had presided over Thomas of Lancaster's mock trial, at which he had again been denied the right to defend himself.

Apparelled in his robes of estate as both knight and earl, Harclay was made to stand for the mere moments that it took Sir Geoffrey le Scrope to read out the charges before the sentence was passed.

'By Order of His Majesty, King Edward Plantagenet the Second of Caernarvon, on this day, the 3rd March, 1323, you Andrew Harclay shall be stripped of your robes, your spurs will be hacked off and your sword shall be broken over your head.'

All this was read while he tried to stop shaking in terror.

'Now we proclaim you no knight, but knave. A traitor who shall have the death of a traitor.'

Without further ado, Harclay was manhandled out of the castle to the great platform and gallows that had been swiftly erected in front of the castle walls, where a huge multitude had gathered to see his greatness ground into the dirt. He recognised many of them, either as servants, labourers on his estates or even some who had fought under his lead. People that he believed he had treated well, whom he had elevated as his own fortunes increased, yet who now were here to witness his death and humiliation. Some swore, others spat and all brayed for his demise.

A black-gowned friar mumbled some words in Latin in front of him and once finished made the sign of the cross before quickly climbing down from the platform, leaving the erstwhile Earl of Carlisle in the hands of the headsman and his assistants.

There was no gentleness in the matter. Like his old benefactor, the Earl of Lancaster, he was not permitted to address the throng, but had his hands roughly bound behind his back. To his horror, he was deprived of a blindfold, for it had been decreed that he would witness his own eventual emasculation and evisceration. A noose was thrown about his neck and pulled tight, and he was hauled up on the gallows and turned as he writhed and struggled to breathe, so that the mob could see his torment and he in turn could see them enjoying the spectacle.

He was hanged until almost dead and then cut down and revived with buckets of water thrown by the headsman's assistants.

After gasping several deep breaths, he cried out a curse. 'I, Andrew Harclay ... curse the King ... curse his man lover Hugh le Despenser... I curse Lancaster, the traitor ... and all his evil... I curse every person with a hand in this, my murder ... and any who defile my body when I have gone.'

The headsman gave him a backhanded blow across the face and pointed at the table with its tools of death. His assistants threw the deposed Earl of Carlisle upon it and roughly removed his clothes to expose his nakedness. Working with great speed as the crowd watched and collectively gasped and groaned, the executioner cut off his genitals, slashed open his abdomen and dragged his bowels out and cast them all into a hot brazier to increase his torment in his last moments of life. Decapitation followed, then the quartering of his body.

As the headsman completed his grisly task and grasped a handful of hair in his blood-covered hand to lift the head and dangle it before the crowd, some said that Harclay's face looked serene. Others pointed to his famously large snub nose and cleft chin and laughed, saying that the haughty bastard had had it all coming.

And among the throng the chatter was of the curse upon the traitorous Harclay, delivered by Thomas the Earl of Lancaster. The fact that their deaths were just a few days short of a year apart, within the time given in the curse, was taken to be of great significance.

Indeed, it had been mere days after Lancaster's death that miracles were reported in his name, and he was not only declared a martyr, but a saintly one. Such was the perfidious nature of the people that even those who had harangued Thomas of Lancaster at his death turned to praise and exalt him but days later.

Now upon Harclay's death, talk of the two curses passed from mouth to mouth in the markets, taverns and churches within the city. The curse of the saintly Thomas of Lancaster was said to have been proven when Andrew Harclay was executed. Yet the whole crowd had heard Harclay's curse after he had been hanged, before the headsman had silenced and then butchered him. That, too, was deemed to be working when one of the headsman's assistants was found dead in an alleyway of Carlisle just two days after the deed, even as the earl's dismembered body parts were being scattered to cities across the realm. Within weeks, talk of the two curses spread far and wide across the country to reach every commoner, lord and lady, passing ever upwards until it reached the Royal Court.

His Majesty, King Edward Plantagenet the Second of Caernarvon was deeply troubled when he heard this, as was his friend and special adviser, Hugh le Despenser, known behind their backs as 'the King's Eye'. Both were outraged at the gossip, but they were also much unsettled by it, for they had each been cursed by the King's cousin, Thomas, the Earl of Lancaster, the saintly martyr. And now they had both been cursed by Andrew Harclay, the erstwhile Earl of Carlisle.

CHAPTER ONE

Pontefract, 28th August, 1323

'Come, my brothers,' said Father Percival, the Prior of the Lazar House. 'It is only a little further and not too much of a climb.'

It had taken the group of lepers a long time to trudge and hobble the mile and a half from the Lazar House in the mud and the rain. There were nine of them, eight men and one woman, all afflicted by the disease that was feared by everyone and which resulted in them being forced to live apart from their fellows until the day they died. Yet these nine were each grateful in some measure that they did not have to live entirely on their own, for they had been fortunate to gain a home and sanctuary in the Lazar House of Pontefract, built and run by the Order of St Lazarus of Jerusalem, otherwise known as the Leper Brothers of Jerusalem.

Yet, as in all things, some were more fortunate than others. Three of them lived there as 'corrody' inmates, having been granted a cell of their own, food and some comfort, thanks to a benefice from one of the holy houses. They had only the lightest of duties and could devote themselves to prayer, rest and eternal hope that they would live out their lives with minimal pain and suffering. Five others had 'cremett' beds, meaning they shared a dormitory cell and were expected to work in the kitchens, gardens and the liquorice fields behind the high walls that separated the Lazar House from the rest of the world.

Father Percival was a leper himself, although his disease was not as far advanced as most of those under his care, even though he was one of the oldest in the Lazar House. He had several patches of pale skin over his face and body, numbness of his feet and a little finger that was crooked. None of it incapacitated him, although he was aware that it would progress. One other was similarly little afflicted, but the rest had all suffered for several years and had discoloured bumps and lumps all over their faces and bodies, some with ulcers and sores which festered and leaked pus so that they had to be heavily bandaged. Many of them had maimed limbs with stumpy, damaged and deformed fingers and toes, partly due to the numbness that made injuries so common with them. Three were deaf and two had lost their sight due to white opacities that had formed on the front of their eyes.

The most infirm, and the one who travelled the slowest, because he had to hop between crutches as he seemed to have but one foot, was called Lucas. Often when he was seen at the crossroads leading into Pontefract, or at the bottom of the Gillygate, two places where he would sometimes place his begging bowl, he would have urchins call names at him, such as Jumping Jack, Lazarus One Leg, or One-legged-toad. All of the lepers were used to such cruel taunts when they went begging, fully aware that each of them was known and feared in Pontefract, yet among themselves none had a nickname. They all knew that the course of the disease was unpredictable even to the shrewdest of physicians, apothecaries or barber surgeons, and there was a strong regard for divine providence. None had any desire to hasten the speed or extent of their suffering or ultimate demise by insulting their fellows. Accordingly, as Father Percival always exhorted them to do, they always turned the other cheek, never retaliated with words, but forced themselves to wish well on others and pray for a cure.

All of them wore sombre grey or brown gowns and hoods. Most either used a staff, stick or leaned on crutches. Hanging from their belts were either small bells or wooden clappers that they used when approaching people to alert them to their presence. Some had thongs with scallop shells strung around their necks, evidence of having previously made pilgrimage to the shrine of St James in Santiago de Compostela in distant Spain in the hope of a cure. Now, all were being led by Father Percival to the shrine of Thomas of Lancaster in the Priory Church of St John the Evangelist in Pontefract.

On the way they had passed the town gibbet from which hung a human-shaped metal cage containing the decaying remains of an executed criminal. Much of the flesh that was not covered by the tattered clothes had been stripped away by crows, and here and there bare bones protruded. Father Percival had muttered some words in Latin and the group all crossed themselves, each silently acknowledging that they were at least better off than the wretch whose remains had been left to be battered by rain and wind and eaten by ravens and crows as an example to all who passed by.

None of them looked closely at the corpse, focusing instead on keeping their feet on the muddy trail and avoiding the puddles as best they could. Because of this, they did not see the man sheltering in a copse of trees beyond the gibbet. Nor did they hear his soft laugh as he watched them, enjoying the sight of their struggle in the rain and mud, especially that of the one he recognised and knew as One-legged-toad, who hopped behind them, swinging his leg between his crutches.

Perkin Cratwell, who was both the public and the royal executioner, often chose this spot to come to observe travellers' reactions as they passed the gibbet and saw his handiwork, which he was so proud of.

The rain came down harder than ever as the leper party reached Pontefract, and after their climb they took the Baileygate around the castle and trudged out along the Ferrybridge road to reach the Monk's Hill, where they could see the high walls and the gates of St John's Priory.

All of them were soaked through, despite their heavy gowns and hoods, but they were thankful that there were fewer people about while the rain fell so heavily. They had used bells and clappers when they saw people, but had received little in the way of abuse or shows of revulsion, which were reactions that they were used to on the occasions they ventured so far from the Lazar House in a big group.

'Look there, my brothers, the cross the monks of St John's Priory erected on the spot where blessed Thomas was slain. There is no one here because of the rain, so you can touch the ground if you wish before we visit the church.'

Everyone took the opportunity to touch the site of the execution and anoint their heads with a dab of the mud. Whatever possible help they could get, they took.

'Will we be permitted to enter the church, Father?' asked Watt of Wetherby, who in his previous life before he was an outcast had been a stonemason who had often worked on churches.

'No, my brother, we have had special dispensation from Prior Stephen of Cherobles, the Prior of St John for us to visit the Priory Church, but we must only use the Lazar window to the side of the nave. A monk will give us each water from a bowl that has been placed over saintly Thomas's tomb.'

Watt sighed with disappointment. 'But at least we can hope that the blessed water may heal us.'

Margaret Fletcher, who had once been counted a rare beauty, but who now wore a bandage around her face to conceal the way her nose had collapsed into the saddle-like deformity that was common with leprosy, tugged at Father Percival's sleeve. 'Is there any chance that we might see the girl that the nun, Sister Esmeralda, told us about? The one who had the vision of saintly Thomas and was given a gift?'

Father Percival smiled at her and put a comforting hand on her shoulder. 'I fear not, Margaret. I understand that she is yet young and is protected by her father.'

'And is ... is she pretty?' Margaret asked.

'That I know not,' he replied, aware that Margaret felt unclean and disgusted by her own appearance as the disease had ravaged her face. 'But if her soul is as lovely as yours, she will be very blessed.' He pointed to a monk standing with his hands in his sleeves in the pouring rain by the gates of the priory. 'Come, my friends. Prior Stephen has sent a monk to guide us.'

Perkin Cratwell was a large man: tall and barrel-chested with muscular arms and large hands. He had a ruddy complexion, cold, dark eyes and a mouth that fell naturally into a downturned scowl. Like his father before him, he had been a butcher with a shop on the Fleshbooths behind Northgate. That was until he followed his uncle and became the public executioner and punisher.

It was work that he excelled in and which he initially did at the same time as his butchery. He learned from his uncle all the fine arts of flogging and hanging, the best types of noose to make according to how he was told to perform the execution.

Break the neck or slow throttle and the jig of death often pleased the crowds, for there was plenty of room at an execution for folk to gamble. Occasionally he carried out the sentence of death by drowning, or by crushing. Folks were less keen on the watery deaths by forced submersion in a barrel, but revelled in seeing him load ever increasing weights onto a raft laid across the victim's chest until ribs cracked and collapsed and breathing stopped. The latter was a death often meted out to outlaws.

Then his uncle died. Fell into the town ditch and broke his neck was how the coroner, Sir Cedric Fairfax — father of the current coroner — had judged it, although there were some that whispered that he had been done away with after he had taught his nephew all that he knew.

Soon after that Perkin Cratwell's fortune changed, and his name and his skill at ending lives reached the ears of the nobility, and even better, of the King. He was given the opportunity of increasing his range of skills by adding the various types of torture that the nobles liked to inflict on their enemies before they were sent to die a horrible death. The animal carcases he butchered were used for practising the disembowelling and the quartering of the body, unbeknownst to his customers. Likewise the dogs he decapitated with his headsman's axe helped him build up his expertise in hitting the exact place on the neck, not too close to the upper two vertebrae, but usually between the third and fourth where there was good mobility and little resistance to the blade. None of his subjects would ever have to suffer the agony of a second swing of the axe, but would have their life snuffed with one blow.

His Majesty King Edward called upon him with increasing frequency to ride around the country to various castles, towns and cities to hang conquered enemies in chains, humiliate them on the scaffold and deal out the traitor's death by hanging, drawing, emasculating and quartering. Even though he wore a leather hood and huge leather apron while using his tools and instruments of death, he became well known across the land. Indeed, everyone in his hometown of Pontefract knew who he was and what he was.

It was fortunate that the King gave him quarters of his own in Pontefract Castle, a regular income as the official royal executioner and granted him the not inconsiderable *droit de havage*, the right of havage, for his butcher's shop on the Fleshbooths had ceased to make him any money. No one in Pontefract wanted to buy meat from Perkin Cratwell anymore.

Gertrude had worked in bawdy houses for almost as long as she could remember, after being sold into service by her father when she first showed signs of becoming a woman. She always counted herself lucky to have had a good instructress in Peggaty and to have found herself in Bardolph's house in one of the nameless backstreets behind Salter's Row, because he was not violent like some of the other bawdy house masters and mistresses. With her naturally cheerful disposition and carnal skills she was one of the most popular prostitutes in the town, much to the chagrin of some of the other strumpets.

She was having a well-earned catnap just after two bells when Bardolph called her.

'Cratwell is here,' he whispered, nervously. 'He wants you again.'

'Why not one of the others?' she asked, plaintively.

'You know how it is. I always ask if he wants to try Kate or Nell, but he chooses you. Maybe you treat him too well.'

'He never wants to be well-treated, master,' she replied with resignation.

She shivered and closed her eyes for several seconds. It was part of her strategy to deal with her revulsion for the man that she had to service whenever he wanted. She knew that as a bawd she had little say in anything. The good women of the town looked down on her whenever she went out, some even spitting on her. As for the men, her customers, they either talked lewdly about her or plain ignored her lest others should realise they had visited Bardolph's bawdy house and paid for their pleasure. But in Perkin Cratwell's case there would be no payment, no pleasure for her, just an act that had to be endured. And all the time she had to feign enjoyment, because she knew that was what men liked to see.

Such was the life of a bawd. Effectively, like Kate and Nell and the others, she was an outcast and had to use her body and wiles just to survive. At least that way she had a roof over her head.

The rain stopped, leaving the streets muddy with large puddles. After leaving the brothel, Perkin Cratwell ambled around the corn and wool markets before making for Baxtergate, where the bakers plied their trade and where he could get a couple of pies to sate the hunger that always followed a session with a bawd.

'I'll have two of your best mutton pies, Samuel,' he said to the slightly portly piemaker. He worked on the principle that a cook or a baker could be trusted to make good food if they had a paunch themselves. As usual, he tapped his purse after taking the pies, although he knew how the man would respond.

'Master Cratwell, don't even think of payment. It is my pleasure, sir. If I know that you enjoy those pies, why, that is payment enough for me.'

The headsman took a mouthful and chewed it well before gracing the pieman with the semblance of a smile. 'It's good,' he said laconically.

'Then I'm a happy man.'

Cratwell nodded and then waited for the folk behind him to move out of his way, as they always would, then set off towards the main marketplace to see if there were any sights worth his attention. As usual, there were peddlers of all sorts and a friar haranguing a small crowd from the base of the Cross of St Oswald. Cratwell stopped and listened for a few moments only, showing his disdain for the friar's message by spitting sideward.

Further on, a juggler dressed in a blue tunic and yellow breeches with a matching blue liripipe was amazing another crowd that had formed behind a band of urchins by tossing an almost impossible number of flasks round and round, so fast that it seemed as if he was barely touching them.

'My friends, I have travelled about the land. I have been to York, Coventry, Cambridge and London. Each one of these flasks holds my wonderful elixir.'

The crowd laughed and clapped at his ever more complicated juggling tricks, as he gyrated, bent and whirled like a human caterpillar. Without stopping, he bent and scooped up another two flasks and flung them up so that he had eight bottles which almost seemed to move up and down in the air of their own volition.

'I have studied the secrets of the greatest physicians and the most skilled apothecaries, and I have mixed up the most wonderful physic that will cure all manner of ailments.'

Up went the bottles in a great high circle, as he tossed them back and forth, catching some behind his back and in the blink of an eye spinning round to keep them up in the air. More people were attracted by the noise and the sight of his juggling.

'Can it grow back my hair?' bellowed a man at the front, whipping off his hat to reveal a shiny bald head.

'Use this every day and by the next harvest you will have had to chop your crop of hair three times.'

'Can it get rid of my cough?'

'What about my old mother's apoplexy?'

'All of these, my friends, for the smallest of costs.'

'What about leprosy?' asked a man in a gown with a hood drawn down over his face.

Immediately the crowd withdrew from around him, but still the juggler kept his circulating flasks in the air. 'Even leprosy,' he said.

The hooded figure suddenly threw back his hood to reveal a perfectly healthy face. 'Then I'll know where to come if I should get it.'

People heaved sighs of relief and then began to laugh.

'So come, friends,' cried the juggler, bending and plucking one flask after the other from the circle and placing them on the ground in front of him until he had a line. 'I have eight flasks of my elixir and a few more in my basket. Who will be first?'

Perkin Cratwell had seen enough of the mountebank at this stage. He thought that the fellow was skilled and good at his work, just as he was good at his. But he was a healthy soul himself and had no need of bottled sheep's piss and honey or whatever else he was peddling. He turned away and made his way through the crowds, stopping at a booth to take a couple of apples. As usual, he was charged nothing at all.

Brother Jean-Claude spoke only a little English despite having lived in the priory for two years, having before that lived as a lay brother in the Abbey in France known as *La Charité-sur-Loire*. He did not want to spend much time with the lepers and waited until they had walked twenty paces before turning and entering the doorway of the Priory Church of St John the Evangelist, from where he pointed to the enclosed tunnel that had been built along the east wall of the church.

'*Vous arretez à la fenêtre,*' he called to Father Percival before scuttling away, perceiving that he had done his duty.

Father Percival made no argument, nor showed any ire or disappointment. He and those under his care were used to such treatment, for they were barred from society by both common and ecclesiastical law. They were not permitted to enter a church, other than their own. He led them along the dark corridor towards the light at the end, which shone from within the church.

Prior Stephen of Cherobles himself was waiting inside with a ewer of water. 'Come close, my friends, and each take the wooden cup to drink some of the water that I shall pour. It has been standing on the tomb and has been blessed.'

Father Percival thanked him and indicated for Margaret Fletcher to come first. She took the wooden cup that had been placed on the stone ledge and waited for the prior to pour a little water into it.

Tears flowed down her cheeks and were immediately absorbed by the bandage over her face. 'Thank you, Father,' she mumbled, her nasal voice quavering as she looked through the Lazar window at the prior and the tomb of Thomas of Lancaster set to the right of the high altar behind him.

'Go in peace, my child. May this blessed water help your soul and your body.'

One by one they filtered past, each envious of the people who were able to enter the church. They, as lepers, even Father Percival himself, had been obliged to undergo the ceremony when they entered the Lazar House.

Margaret Fletcher remembered her ceremony only too well, when she'd been led to the altar of their church and exhorted to suffer with a patient and penitent spirit the incurable plague with which God had stricken her. Father Percival had sprinkled her with holy water, all the while reading aloud the Burial Service, for indeed she was effectively dead to the living.

Then her clothes were taken away and she was enveloped in a pall, and placed between two trestles, like a corpse, before the altar, when the Libera was sung and the Mass of the Dead was celebrated over her. After that, she was formally admitted to the Lazar House, her home until she died. Like all the other lepers, now depersonalised in everything except her name, she was given her clappers, a bell and the leper's clothes: a russet tunic, and a gown with sleeves that covered the hands and a hem that reached the ankles.

From then on, life was prayer, penitence, work and waiting. Each morning they would all say a Paternoster and Ave Maria thirteen times. Every hour after, in between whatever work or study was given to them, they would say the same prayers seven times more, and then before every meal they would say prayers for the Order of St Lazarus and for St Mary Magdalene.

Lucas took his turn at the window and gratefully received his water and blessing. As he turned, one of his crutches skidded on the ground and he went over slightly on his ankle, only being stopped from falling by Father Percival.

'Are you all right, my son?' asked Prior Stephen, peering concernedly through the Lazar window.

'I thank you, fathers,' Lucas replied to both men. 'It may swell, but I will rest it when I get back home. The one blessing of our disease is that I rarely feel pain in the parts of the body that are most crippled.'

Father Percival took his water last of all, thanked the prior and then led his charges back to their Lazar House. Fortunately, the rain had stopped.

There were thirteen taverns and hostelries in Pontefract and Perkin Cratwell gave each of them his trade. Or rather, he drank as much ale as he wanted in them for free. He never visited the same one two nights in a row, but usually took two mugs in one with a meal and then several more in a second. This evening, he had eaten at the Pikestaff before visiting the Mulberry Bush, near the Church of St Giles. The curfew hour never bothered him, for none of the night watch would dare to approach him. It was another of the special freedoms that he enjoyed in Pontefract.

A fire burned in the hearth and there were many men drinking at the tables as he entered the smoky atmosphere of the Mulberry. He heard the calling out of bets and numbers, followed by the clack and rattle of rolling dice.

Snapping his fingers at the landlord, he pointed to the table from whence all the commotion was coming and advanced upon it. A space was immediately created for him and a mug of ale was set before him.

'My pleasure, Master Cratwell,' the landlord responded with a shake of the head when the headsman touched his purse.

He cast an eye round the group of gamblers, recognising the juggler he had seen earlier. They were playing Hazard, and the juggler was the caster. Judging by the pile of coins in front of him and the correspondingly meagre amounts in front of the other players, he was good at it.

'Do you play Hazard, Master Cratwell?' asked a timid-looking fellow who Cratwell knew to be a tailor called Brattle.

'I'll play,' he replied, taciturnly. He reached into his purse and drew out a pile of coins, which he neatly piled in front of him.

He waited until the caster started to lose. When he had lost three times in a row, he handed the dice to Brattle, who thought for a moment then cried out: 'Seven! My main is seven.'

The players all made their bets while the tailor eagerly fingered the dice. When all bets were on, he blew on them for luck, shook them then tossed them. They rolled and stopped, showing a three and a four.

'I win!' he declared.

He followed it with a five and a two on the next game, and won. Then with a six and two, which was called a 'chance' so he rolled again, but then lost. He lost twice more and with a wry smile withdrew from the game and handed the dice to Perkin Cratwell.

The games proceeded and several more mugs of ale were drunk, with Cratwell losing some and winning others, as did the juggler until there were only the two of them left. All the others drank up and left them to it. At last, after returning from the yard outside to relieve his bladder, Perkin Cratwell found another mug of ale waiting for him.

'This drink is on me, my friend,' said the juggler, raising his mug in a toast. 'Between the two of us, I think we lightened the other players' purses considerably.'

Cratwell laughed as they chinked mugs. 'You play well, master juggler. I saw you earlier and admired your skill with those flasks, though I wasn't convinced that they contained the wondrous physic you said they did.' He took a hefty swig of ale and wiped his mouth with the back of his hand. 'Tell me, what is your name?'

'Gladwin of Middleham, sir,' the entertainer replied. 'I thank you; as an actor, I have picked up some juggling and conjuring skills along the way. With regard to my Hazard playing, why, I simply understand numbers more than most. When I am the caster, I know which numbers give me the best chance of rolling my main, and when I am a player I bet when I think I have a better chance of the caster missing. I suspect you use the same tactics.'

Perkin Cratwell thumped the table with his fist. 'And I thought I was the only one who had puzzled it out. Mayhap there is more to your elixir than I thought, after all.' He suddenly felt hot and wiped a patina of perspiration from his brow. 'This ale must be stronger than usual. Mayhap it is a fresh firkin.'

The juggler laughed. 'Or the bottom of an old hogshead. But we were talking about my elixir. I assure you, sir, it is the finest physic you could have. I use only the best ingredients.'

'I thought you would say something like that,' returned Cratwell with a laugh. 'So you are an actor and a juggler. One of the outcasts.' He used his mug to gesture at the empty seats around them. 'Like me. As you can see, I can clear a space anywhere. People know me, play dice with me, but will take the opportunity to leave as soon as they can. Gladwin of Middleham, you see before you one of the greatest outcasts.'

Gladwin of Middleham laughed. 'And I thought it was because we were better Hazard players than they. As for myself, as an actor, like you say, some would call us outcasts, but I would prefer to call myself an artist. Your name, sir?'

'Perkin Cratwell.' He suddenly felt a spasm of pain and put a hand on his gut.

The juggler eyed him shrewdly. 'Well, Perkin, I think that you must be either the landlord's very own brother or someone extremely important, like the royal executioner.'

Perkin Cratwell raised an eyebrow suspiciously. 'I take it someone told you when I was at the market.'

'Not at all. I would have to be blind not to notice that whereas I and every other player paid for our drinks, though you always tap your purse, you actually sup for free. I also saw in the market when you left that you obtained two apples and again paid nothing. That implies to me that you have *droit de havage*.'

'Aye, I am the royal executioner,' Cratwell admitted, before belching loudly. 'King Edward in his grace gave me havage, so I may impose tax on any merchant or seller of anything that I buy. The people of Pontefract consider it simplest to just forego payment on anything I choose.'

Gladwin of Middleham leaned forward with his elbows on the table and lowered his voice. 'Tell me, Perkin, is it true that a piece of the rope you hang a man with has the power to cure headaches and all afflictions of the throat?'

Perkin Cratwell blinked as he contemplated his ale. Perspiration was forming in beads on his forehead, and his cheeks had suddenly reddened. 'Aye, that and ... and more. It will cure all types of pains, choking fits and the like.'

'Could you sell me a piece, Perkin?'

The headsman said nothing for a moment, but gulped as if holding back some vomit. Then, without warning, he rose from the table and ran for the door.

Outside, in the darkness of the midden yard behind the Mulberry Bush, he fell to his knees and vomited. He clutched his belly and felt as if his bowels were about to squirt. He did not hear footsteps behind him.

A loop of rope dropped over his neck as he was retching. He barely noticed it. It was not until a foot in his back forced him to the ground and the rope tightened to cut off his air that he realised he was about to die.

It was close to midnight when the gong wagon carrying the night soil from the town's cesspits, middens, pits and dumps trundled along the North Baileygate, ready to be transported out of town. By the time it reached the north gate, the guards had opened the barriers so that the two gong farmers could take their foetid load through as quickly as possible.

'Going far tonight?' one of the guards called.

'To Ferrybridge. We have a load for the fields near the Stump Cross.'

No one ever searched the gong wagons.

CHAPTER TWO

Wakefield, 6th September, 1323

Tarbet of Lupset, the swineherd, rubbed his heavily stubbled chin and swallowed hard, his prominent Adam's apple bobbing up and down to show his nervousness.

'I can't pay, Your Honour. I've no money left,' he said, patting the empty purse hanging from his belt.

An impatient murmur rose from the crowd as they turned their heads en masse away from the man in the dock and gazed up at Sir Richard Lee sitting behind the high bench to see his reaction.

'You should not have spent it on getting yourself so drunk,' Sir Richard replied, sternly.

'My wife and son both died this spring, Your Honour. I drink to forget.'

John of Flanshaw, the court bailiff, raised his hand to catch Sir Richard's attention. When the judge nodded at him, he stood up from his stool and addressed the accused swineherd. 'You drank so much that you forgot that you needed to pay William Farrow the baker for a loaf of bread. That's stealing.'

'A man has to eat,' returned Tarbet of Lupset sourly.

More impatient whisperings rose from the crowd.

Sir Richard sighed and adjusted the lawyer's coif upon his head and leaned forward. He had some sympathy for the man, but the facts were clear: the swineherd had stolen a loaf from the baker's shop on the Westgate, after having drunk several mugs of ale in at least five local taverns.

'Tarbet of Lupset,' he said, 'you have broken the law and committed theft of a loaf. The fine I imposed on you is a lenient sentence, considering that I could have you pilloried. I acknowledge the fact that you have lost both your wife and son, hence my lenience. Now you say that you have sold your pigs and foolishly drunk the money away.'

More murmurings of anticipation from around the court caused Sir Richard to frown and rap his gavel on the desk.

'Silence while the judge speaks!' John of Flanshaw called out. Immediately, all noise ceased.

'I understand from John of Flanshaw that you have never been in trouble before and that until your family died, you were not a drunkard. I am going to be yet more lenient and give you the opportunity to work your debt off. You will help muck out the stables and tend to the swine at Sandal Castle until you earn enough to pay William Farrow the price of three loaves plus the fine of two groats to the court.'

The swineherd had been clutching his hat in his hands. At the judge's words, he heaved a sigh of relief and tugged his forelock. 'I thank you, Your Honour. I...'

'And you will refrain from drinking while you are so employed. You may take a seat in the court and see the bailiff afterwards to receive instructions and a message to take to Sandal Castle.'

Once again, there were mutterings of disappointment from about the court. Sir Richard knew that many considered him over-lenient.

Sir Richard Lee had spent all morning hearing cases at the Manor Court, which was held in the Wodehalle, as the Moot Hall was known in Wakefield. It was a large timber-framed building capable of holding up to two hundred people, a number that it almost always reached, as absence at the Manor Court was punishable with a fine. There was generally not a lot of enthusiasm for the court unless there was some serious case to be considered, such as a murder, a public outrage or serious robbery, all of which could receive a punishment worth attention. Mere incarceration or a fine did not enthuse people, but the possibility of some sport with an unfortunate offender sentenced to time in the stocks or pillory, a birching or better still a hanging, brought folk in their droves, eager for a seat as close to the dais upon which the judge and jury sat, and the wooden enclosure in which the accused stood.

This interest in punishment versus indifference to judgements on more mundane matters had been Richard's impression of the attendees' attitude at the Manor Courts when he first arrived in Wakefield two years previously, appointed by the King himself. Prior to this, the Wakefield Manor Court had been held by Sir Thomas Deyville, the Steward of the Manor of Wakefield, a man who had a very different idea of justice to Richard. As Sir Thomas was not versed in law, he had dispensed what he considered to be appropriate sentences, such as public floggings, duckings in horse troughs, or immersions in barrels of urine. He had only stopped short at the putting out of eyes or the amputation of thumbs by the good counsel of some of the town elders and the priests of the local parishes, who had petitioned him together.

Richard had initially made himself unpopular with Sir Thomas when he assumed control of the Manor Court, for he was determined to change the way that the law was delivered and perceived. He believed fervently in justice for all, and wanted people to feel that the law was there to protect them, no matter their position, and that it was fair to all. It was, as he knew only too well, an aspiration that was not easy to attain, for injustice abounded throughout the land.

The animosity of Sir Thomas would not have worried Richard overmuch if he had not been forced to stay at Sandal Castle, ostensibly as a guest of the Steward. Then the fact that Sir Thomas had a comely daughter and Cupid had smitten both Richard and her with the arrows of love created a further complication. Now betrothed to be married, Richard had bought an old manor house outside the village of Durkar, a short ride to the south of the castle. Once they were wed, he hoped that he and Lady Wilhelmina would settle and live happily in the manor house and, if the good Lord was willing, would someday have children of their own.

He waited until John of Flanshaw finished writing at his small desk and then called to him. 'Let us hear the last case.'

The bailiff stood and called out in a loud voice, 'Bring in Gideon of Ackworth!'

A door at the side of the dais opened and Hubert of Loxley came in, holding by the arm a shabby-looking fellow with a lean and aggressive demeanour. A large bruise was evident on his jaw, which Richard knew had been given to him by Hubert when he had arrested him that morning after being alerted by Ralph Sutton the blacksmith.

Hopeful noises circulated around the crowd, for everyone had heard what had happened.

Hubert positioned the accused in the dock and stood to the side with his arms folded. His robust presence made it clear that any trouble from the accused would likely result in a cuffing or another bruise. After the bailiff had announced the case for the benefit of the twelve jurors and the crowd, Richard instructed him to call the accuser.

A small man, barely over five foot, dressed in a knee-length, brown monk's habit and sandals and with a rope tied about his narrow waist came forward upon hearing his name, tapping the floor in front of him with a wooden staff. His eyes were wide open but unmoving, and it was clear that if he had vision, it was relatively poor. He reached out in front of him as he approached the bench and touched its edge, then stood still.

'Name yourself,' Sir Richard ordered.

'I am Timothy of Halifax, Your Honour.'

'Are you in holy orders?'

'No, sir. I am a wool merchant, but am now on a pilgrimage to Pontefract.'

'To Pontefract? Do you mean that you are going to stay at Pontefract on your way to York or to Beverley?'

The man shook his head and smiled, revealing a large gap between his front teeth. In a proud voice, he announced, 'No, sir, I go to seek solace from my ills at the tomb of the sainted Thomas.'

This was greeted by many gasps and whisperings from the crowd and the jurors.

'You mean at the tomb of Thomas, Earl of Lancaster?' Richard asked.

Timothy of Halifax nodded enthusiastically. 'Yes, sir, at the tomb of the martyred Thomas, Earl of Lancaster.' He genuflected and made the sign of the cross over his heart.

Richard did not pursue the fact that the Earl of Lancaster was not a saint, or even one who had been canonised, but had died a convicted traitor. 'You go for solace for your ills? What ills? Are you blind, Timothy of Halifax?'

'No, Your Honour. Not entirely, but my eyes grow dimmer by the day so that on some days I can barely see anything but shadows. I am fortunate that I have sons who can look after my business, so that I can go on my pilgrimage, which has not been easy. If it was not for my staff, my good donkey and the kindness of those I meet along the way, I would not get far. I go seeking a miracle, such as many have already received.'

'Tell the court what mishap brought you here?'

Timothy raised his hands in a gesture of helplessness. 'A man met me as I was riding my donkey on the road into Wakefield and walked along with me for a mile or so before he suddenly attacked me, knocked me unconscious and stole my donkey. When I recovered, I found that he had stolen my most precious possession, my pilgrimage badge. I had it specially cast in silver and blessed by my local priest. I take it to be blessed at Pontefract Priory at sainted Thomas's tomb.'

Richard nodded to John of Flanshaw, who produced a large silver badge. He took it over to the pilgrim and placed it in his hands.

'Is this your pilgrimage badge?' Richard asked.

Timothy of Halifax felt it and held it up close in front of him. 'Yes, your honour. It bears images, each depicting an instant in Thomas's blessed life, ending with his martyrdom in front of his own castle at Pontefract and above it two angels carrying his soul to heaven.'

People in the crowd grew restless, craning their necks for a better view of the badge. Richard signalled for it to be brought to him to examine. It was just as Timothy of Halifax described.

He placed it on the bench in front of him. 'It is skilfully made. It will be returned to you later.' Turning to the man in the dock, he continued, 'What say you to this, Gideon of Ackworth?'

'He lies, Your Honour. I was going about my business when this oaf manhandled me!' He glared at Hubert, who unfolded his arms and glared back.

'What say you to this, Hubert of Loxley?' Richard asked.

Hubert stood straight and tall. 'I was in the market when I heard the hue and cry. People were crying out "thief" and "wolf" and screaming. I ran in the direction of the springs near the Church of All Saints where the clamour was coming from. Riding on a donkey through the crowd, kicking aside anyone who tried to stop him, I saw this fellow. Ralph Sutton the blacksmith was there, bent over with his hands on his knees, out of breath from the chase. He told me that the rogue had tried to get him to melt down that charm that you have there and halve it with him. Several folk saw him try to make off on the donkey after Ralph refused, and Ralph raised the hue and cry.'

'He lies, Your Honour. I kicked no one and was on my own donkey.'

Hubert scowled at him again, then turned to carry on. 'I was able to catch up with him before he reached the Northgate. He tried to resist arrest, so I persuaded him of the folly of his ways. He was carrying that talisman inside his hood.'

After calling the blacksmith, Ralph Sutton, who confirmed Hubert's testimony and gave his own, Richard addressed the jurors. 'So you have heard the evidence; do you find this man, Gideon of Ackworth, guilty or not guilty of theft of this pilgrim's badge and his donkey and of causing him bodily harm?'

Timothy of Halifax piped up. 'Your Honour, I wish him no harm. If I could just have my badge, I will continue with my pilgrimage.'

A chorus of amazed disapproval went around the hall.

'Interesting,' Richard mused, rubbing his chin. 'I admire and respect your humility, Timothy of Halifax, yet the law is the law, and I do not feel that this miscreant should escape justice. He needs to be taught that the law is here for a purpose.'

'Birch the dog!' someone called out.

'Hang him!' yelled another.

Richard rapped his gavel and John of Flanshaw cried out for silence, emphasising the point by picking up his staff and banging it on his desk.

'Your pilgrim's badge will be returned, Timothy of Halifax. As for Gideon of Ackworth, it is my decision that you shall be referred to the Ecclesiastical Court, since the theft of the pilgrim's badge, which had been blessed by a parish priest, makes this a moral crime. We shall send word to the York Consistory Court.'

Gideon of Ackworth leered, clearly pleased to be tried by what many considered a softer court.

'Until then,' Sir Richard went on, 'you will be kept in the town pillory from morning until sunset, then incarcerated in the town gaol.'

The crowd spontaneously began to cheer and laugh, much to the miscreant's discomfiture.

After closing the court session, Richard and Hubert went down the long corridor beyond the courtroom to a locked room called the Rolls' Office, which was furnished with a desk and chair and several stools. Taking up a corner of the room was a large, locked chest with numerous pigeonholes, containing the Manor of Wakefield court rolls. Dating back to 1274 and written in a mix of English and Latin on fine vellum scrolls, they recorded all the dealings of the Manor Court.

Richard sat at the table while John of Flanshaw, the bailiff of the Manor Court, carefully inscribed on a vellum sheet the proceedings of the court session as dictated by Richard.

Hubert sat rocking back and forth on a stool on the other side of the room, idly carving a small piece of wood into the shape of a head with his dagger. He intended to add a body and limbs and tie them together with cord to make a doll for his young son. Later, he would make another so that the dolls could be made to wrestle each other. He could not wait until his baby son was old enough for him to teach him the skills that would equip him for manhood.

While he waited for the bailiff to finish writing, Richard glanced at Hubert and smiled. 'Is that a toy for your boy?'

Hubert beamed. 'It is, my lord. You should see how strong his grip is already. Why, he can —' He stopped abruptly, seeing the almost sad smile on his master's lips, which made him think of the tragedies that Richard had lived through and which in a way had forged a link between the two men forever.

'It is shaping well, Hubert,' Richard said. 'Keep carving.'

Richard was thirty-three years of age and had been a Sergeant-at-Law for seven years. Those had been hard times, for he had married Eleanor, Sir Jasper of Loxley's daughter, only to lose her when she died in childbirth. Their baby son had followed her mere days later, and he had plunged into a fit of melancholy, which he was able to assuage by working at law and hunting and learning skills in weaponry from his good and faithful servant, Hubert of Loxley. Formerly one of Sir Jasper's men-at-arms, Hubert entered Sir Richard's service upon his betrothal to Eleanor, when he had been assigned to escort her and stay as her personal bodyguard. After Eleanor's death, the bond between Richard and Hubert had strengthened far beyond that of master and servant.

Like so many other scholars, Richard had also seen the brutality of war, when he answered his sovereign's call and took up arms to fight against the Marcher Lords at Hereford, Pembroke and Shrewsbury. Later still, he had been involved in the rout of the Earl of Lancaster's army at Boroughbridge, as they tried to cross the River Ure.

He had been assigned a troop of his own with Hubert at his right hand. Seemingly without fear after losing Eleanor, Richard had led from the front. Unfortunately, an arrow had caught him in the left calf, penetrating his leg greave and the muscle to embed itself in his horse's belly, so it fell, literally pinning him under it. At the mercy of Lancaster's infantry with their bollock daggers, which were used to slit the throat or slip inside the helmet eye slits of unhorsed knights, he was saved by Hubert's timely intervention as he dispatched two assailants singlehandedly.

After the battle, Sir Andrew Harclay had been much impressed with Richard and mentioned him in his despatch to the King. He arranged for Richard to be taken to the Abbey of St Mary in York, where he lay raving in the hospital with pain and fever for two weeks. When he recovered, there was Hubert watching over him, ever suspicious of the potions that the Benedictine monks were wont to ply him with. When he was sufficiently recovered, Hubert gave him the sealed orders from the King himself, requesting his presence at York Castle when he was sufficiently recovered.

It was then, in a private audience with King Edward, that he was given his special commission as Circuit Judge of the King's Northern Realm and Judge of the Manor of Wakefield Court. That had been the start of their laborious and lengthy round of all the towns and villages in the area of the Manor of Wakefield and the Honour of Pontefract.

Coming to Wakefield had been beneficial for both Richard and Hubert. Richard had fallen in love with Lady Wilhelmina and planned to marry later in the year. Hubert had fallen for Beatrice Quigley, the buxom owner of the Bucket Inn within the town of Wakefield. Richard had given his blessing for Hubert to marry, and they already had a sturdy, bouncing boy.

Having finished his dictation, Richard gave John of Flanshaw some further instructions and the bailiff left to carry them out. While Richard sat writing some notes of his own on a fresh sheet of parchment, Hubert tidied the wood carvings and stowed the small wooden doll in his doublet.

The sound of shuffling feet accompanied by heavy boots hurriedly coming along the corridor was followed by a knock at the door.

'Come in,' called Richard.

The door slowly opened, and one of the court ushers deferentially entered. He looked hesitantly over his shoulder and then turned to address Richard. 'A messenger has come asking for you, Sir Richard. Not just a … a messenger, if it please you, but a … a royal messenger.'

A gauntleted hand landed on the usher's shoulder and moved him aside as a man in royal livery stepped into the room. He swept off his hat and bowed.

'Sir Richard Lee, I bring a message from His Majesty, King Edward.' He took two quick steps forward and produced a message from his tunic. He held it out across the desk.

Hubert abruptly stopped his rocking and stood up, his interest piqued.

Richard opened the message and straightened it out to read it. His eyes widened and he nodded. 'I thank you. I suggest that you return to the castle and tell His Majesty that we will follow you directly, once I have dealt with a few urgent court matters.'

The King's messenger said nothing but bowed again, spun on his heel and instantly marched back along the corridor. His function was to deliver his sovereign's messages as swiftly as possible and to speak only when directed to do so. There was no question of him waiting to ride with Sir Richard; he needed to return to the King and inform him that the message had been delivered, read and was about to be acted upon.

After the messenger and the court usher had gone, Hubert watched Richard re-read the message. He noted the bemused expression on his master's face. 'A message from the King, my lord? Is there some mystery in it?'

'King Edward has arrived at Sandal Castle, and he and his special adviser await my presence. The King wants my counsel and my skills.'

'The King and the King's Eye?' Hubert said, frowning as he scratched his smoothly shaven cheek. 'They want your counsel, my lord? Surely that is an honour?'

Richard gave a hollow laugh. 'Perhaps it is, Hubert. Yet the King is not one known to either seek or listen to counsel from anyone but his own chamberlain. You asked if there is mystery in it, and I would say there is. He says it concerns the scourge of curses and pilgrims in his realm. And of murder.'

CHAPTER THREE

Wakefield was a straggling town of gabled wooden houses, thatched with reeds or straw. Those dwellings or businesses with two storeys all had undercrofts on the ground floor for keeping their animals or storing their supplies. There were three main streets, all of which were rutted by oxcarts and packhorses and had side streets and alleys leading off them. Richard and Hubert walked their horses towards the marketplace from the Wodehalle, passing open doors from whence emanated odours of woodsmoke, baking bread and cooking. And then as they approached the marketplace, the stench of dung overpowered the other smells.

'We shall have to get John of Flanshaw to have stern words with the reeves and burghers about these dung heaps,' said Richard, nodding at several large hillocks of dung and offal.

'Aye, my lord. I will take him to task, for they are unpleasant to the nose and have been allowed to grow too high and stay overlong. The gong farmers will likely have several nights carting to do.'

Loud laughter ahead of them suggested that something else other than the usual banter and bargaining was going on at the marketplace.

'At least there is something that our court bailiff did not tarry over,' Hubert said with a grim smile. 'He has made the people happy and given them some sport.'

Already locked in the public pillory, his head and wrists secured in the holes, Gideon of Ackworth was being pelted with clods of dung and rotten vegetables by a crowd of urchins. At a sign from Richard, Hubert shouted at them.

Catching sight of the Manor Court judge's man, they dispersed into the market crowds, like mice fleeing from a cat.

'My lord, look at that tooth-puller,' said Hubert, pointing to a crowd around a mountebank's crude stage as they urged their horses through the busy marketplace. A flag bearing the likeness of St Apollonia hung from a pole, and beneath it a man wearing an apron was waving a pair of small iron tongs in one hand and a strange multi-armed tool in his other.

'My friends, I can take teeth out with absolutely no pain, thanks to this wonderful new tool that the French have just created, called a Pelican. I travelled to Paris myself to buy one and learn its use, so that I can ease the suffering of my fellow men. Come now, who will be next?'

Hubert laughed as they passed on. 'He has a way with words, and by the look of the people and the number clutching their jaws, he is going to have many customers.'

'Let us just thank St Apollonia that we're spared his tongs or his Pelican.'

'I don't like those tools he uses,' Hubert said with a wince. 'They are like the barbaric things the executioners use. Like they did on our poor commander, Sir Andrew Harclay.'

They turned in their saddles at a cry of pain, in time to see a wriggling customer in a chair struggling as the mountebank tooth-puller rested a knee on his chest and pulled a bloody yellow tooth with the Pelican and tongs. The crowd applauded, laughed and groaned all at the same time as the performer neatly tossed the offending tooth into a bucket as he stuffed a rag into his patient's mouth before taking a bow.

'He is fast, if not exactly painless,' said Richard. 'But see how people like to see blood, Hubert. The tooth-puller yanking out teeth on his stage and the executioner exacting pain and humiliation on the scaffold; they are not so different, one is just more spectacular and final than the other.'

Having weaved their way past the marketplace, they rode down the Kirkgate, on their way passing groups of merchants, itinerants and shepherds herding their flocks to the wool market on Birch Hill, then passed the King's Mill, one of the soke mills within the town of Wakefield, and crossed the great timber-buttressed bridge over the River Calder.

Once again they were struck by the stench of the tallow works, so important to the manufacture of precious candles, which was accompanied by the eye-watering smell of boiling horse urine from the tanneries that lined the south bank of the river. It was so bad yet so familiar that they immediately covered their noses and mouths with their neckcloths and urged their mounts to speed up the gently rising, meandering road towards the village of Sandal Magna.

'Have you an idea what murder His Majesty wants to see you about with such urgency, my lord?'

Richard shook his head. 'I have no idea. But it is intriguing, him talking about the scourge of pilgrims when I just saw one in the court.'

'Perhaps he has taken against pilgrims, my lord. In that case they all need to take care, for it is as well not to get on his bad side, as did our poor lord, Sir Andrew Harclay.' He touched a hand to his chest and shook his head. 'I doubt if even my arrowhead could have helped him, had I been able to give him it.'

Sir Richard nodded. 'I am sure that you are right, Hubert. Your arrowhead may be able to divert arrows and protect you in battle, but the ire of the all-powerful king would likely not be subdued.'

Richard knew that his man had absolute faith in the arrowhead that he wore on a chain about his neck. Several groats had passed hands when he purchased it, believing it had power to deflect arrows and sword thrusts. The fellow who had sold it to him had said that it had been taken from the back of a crusader at the Siege of Antioch. Richard had once asked how it could deflect such things if it had not done so for the crusader, mere moments before they had actually had arrows fired at them by the outlaw Robin Hood and his men. None had hit them, of course, since they were merely warning shots, but afterwards Hubert had taken this as further proof of the arrowhead's power. On several occasions after that, Hubert had escaped death from arrows, daggers and sword, so Richard had decided it was better to be pragmatic and leave Hubert with his belief in his amulet, and so the unknown slain crusader was never mentioned by either of them again.

They were about the same age. Sir Richard knew that he was exactly thirty-three years of age, and Hubert had an idea that he was round about that many years. Richard was tall and well-built with a mane of raven black hair and a short well-groomed beard, as befitted his position and class. He had piercing blue eyes and a well chiselled albeit slightly bent nose, having broken it in a joust some years before. Hubert was also tall, but thicker set and had brown hair and laughing brown eyes. He shaved his beard every Saturday and had cheeks that became round when he laughed, which was frequently.

They had travelled in silence since crossing the river, and Hubert was in the mood to express his thoughts. 'What you said back there, my lord — about the tooth-puller and the executioner — it set me thinking. I can hardly believe that it is half a year since we heard the news about Sir Andrew. I mean, with him having been made Earl of Carlisle after the Battle of

Boroughbridge, it seemed so unjust that he should fall out of favour with the King and be executed in such a horrible manner. Hanged, drawn and quartered!'

'The law can be brutal, Hubert. I often feel that some laws and punishments should be changed, but I am not in a position to do that. As a lawyer, I must serve the law.'

After a moment, Hubert said, 'I am glad I did not see the execution. I know part of him was kept in Carlisle, but where were his other parts taken, my lord?'

Richard grimaced. 'His head was boiled in tar and taken to Knaresborough Castle, where the King was staying, before it was put on a spike above Tower Bridge in London. The other quartered parts were nailed to the gates of Carlisle, Newcastle, Bristol and Dover. It was the sentence demanded by the law for treason against the King.'

'And that was only a year after the Earl of Lancaster had been beheaded at Pontefract. At least Thomas of Lancaster had been spared the debasement of the disembowelling and being cut into pieces like a carcass of beef or pork, with him being of royal blood. Yet I am sure it must have been the curse, my lord. And on the scaffold just before he died, Harclay himself cursed the Earl of Lancaster and —'

Richard held up his hand. 'Enough, Hubert. You know I don't believe in that curse any more now than I did when it was first reported.'

'But, my lord, almost a year to the day! Surely, that tells —'

'It tells nothing, Hubert. Sir Andrew Harclay acted rashly in negotiating with Robert the Bruce without His Majesty's knowledge or permission. I personally think he did so in good faith, but our King considered it treason, so a traitor's death was his fate. I wish it had been anything but that, for I do not believe that justice was done that day, yet the King is the King and we his subjects must obey. Otherwise there would be rebellion, and this country has had enough of bloodshed and the like.'

They passed the Sandal Magna village church of St Helen's and started on the final climb towards the sandstone ridge upon which Sandal Castle stood. It was a natural stronghold with clear views over the surrounding countryside. The castle itself was an impressive sight, with its ashlar stones glistening in the afternoon light. A great keep with four circular towers crested an impressive motte, and a battlemented twenty-foot-high curtain wall with turrets at regular intervals along it surrounded a large bailey. The wall crossed the large moat on either side, ascending the slopes of the motte to abut the keep. Protruding above the walls within the curtain wall could be seen the roofs of its splendid halls and the numerous dwellings on the bailey, and the tops of a central barbican and nearby drum towers connecting to the keep.

Hanging from the flagpole atop the keep was the royal standard instead of the usual colours of the Earl of Surrey, the owner of the castle.

As the track wound up to the top of the ridge, they approached the outer defensive earthwork behind which was the large moat. Armed soldiers were visible, looking down upon them from the battlements. As Richard and Hubert were recognised, orders were called out and by the time they had ridden along the embankment to the gatehouse the drawbridge had been lowered and the portcullis raised to allow them entry.

Once inside the castle, the porter signalled to someone in the gatehouse and the portcullis was lowered again. He whistled and instantly an ostler hurried round the corner to take their horses.

'Never known such a day, Sir Richard,' Lorn the porter said, clearly more flustered than usual. 'I can hardly believe that His Majesty King Edward and the royal chamberlain, Lord Hugh le Despenser and all his party have come to Sandal Castle. There must be over a hundred of them! The King's messenger just came back and went to report to them in the Great Hall with Sir Thomas.'

He raised his shoulders and grimaced apologetically. 'Sir Thomas ordered me to tell you to go over as soon as you arrive, but Lady Alecia also told me to tell you that she and Lady Wilhelmina would like to see you before you go across.' He took a deep breath. 'There, Sir Richard, I've told you what I was told to tell you by Sir Thomas and Lady Alecia, so you can decide which —'

'I will see Lady Alecia and Lady Wilhelmina, Lorn,' Richard cut in.

He turned to Hubert. 'I suggest that you go across to the kitchens and get some food. It is many hours since we broke our fast, and I heard your stomach rumble as we rode here.'

Hubert grinned. 'In that case, my lord, I shall make sure that I get extra cheese, bread and a pair of pigeon pies, for you have not supped either.' His eyes twinkled. 'And mayhap a skin of ale.'

Richard went straight to the Steward's House, the first tall building on the large bailey, opposite the inner moat of the castle and the drawbridge that crossed it to the barbican. Normally, the bailey courtyard was thrumming with people, livestock and all manner of activity. The royal visit, however, had caused the chickens and animals to be rounded up and herded into the undercrofts, while the servants bustled about. The guards were stationed at strategic points about the bailey and battlement walls. Richard noted in addition that guards in the royal livery had formed a strong presence around the Great Hall. He had no doubt that the King's entourage would be taking refreshments of fine food and wine in the Lesser Hall, and the rest of the King's guards would be partaking of beer and plainer fare in the kitchens.

Lady Alecia, a middle-aged matron in a shapeless grey gown and wimple, was sitting in her usual high wooden chair close to the burning log fire in the hall of the Steward's house. The day had been reasonably warm for the month, yet despite that a fire was kept blazing in the large grate. Richard knew that the heat was one of the best things to ease the rheumatics that she suffered from. Still a handsome woman, he had a great deal of time for her, knowing that life with her husband, Sir Thomas Deyville, could never be easy. She was a shrewd lady, and he was ever grateful that she had championed his cause when he first began to woo her daughter, Lady Wilhelmina.

'We must not keep you overlong, Richard,' she said as he kissed her hand, careful not to squeeze too hard over the marble-like nodules that made her joints so painful.

Richard nodded gratefully. 'I cannot keep His Majesty waiting more than a few minutes more.'

'Although I would have him wait all day if I could just keep you for an hour or two,' said Wilhelmina, springing off her chair on the other side of the fire and throwing her arms about his neck to kiss him on the lips.

'Wilhelmina,' he whispered. 'Your mother —'

His fiancée wrinkled her nose. 'Oh, Mother doesn't mind me showing affection, Richard. We are both afraid that His Majesty may be about to send you off somewhere dangerous and deprive us of your company.'

'Wilhelmina is right, Sir Richard. Why else would he visit unannounced and send for you immediately upon his arrival?'

Lady Alecia gave an affirmative nod. 'And she is quite correct about displays of affection. Love should not be subdued, as I know full well.'

Richard smiled at his future mother-in-law, realising that she was referring to her own relationship with the bluff Sir Thomas Deyville, so took the opportunity to kiss Wilhelmina again. Then, taking her hand, he turned to Lady Alecia. 'Send me somewhere dangerous, Lady Alecia? Why should you think such a thing?'

The ghost of a smile crossed Lady Alecia's lips. 'Everywhere in England is dangerous these days, Richard. Wakefield is not the idyllic haven it once was, and as we all know, not even Sandal Castle has been without its intrigues.'

Richard nodded with a wan smile, for the last time King Edward had visited Wakefield to see the Mystery Plays performed, Richard had uncovered many malign goings-on.

'I am grateful for your concerns, ladies, yet you know that if the King commands me to go somewhere then perforce I must go, for it will be my duty. But fear not for my safety; as a Sergeant-at-Law and the Circuit Judge of the King's Northern Realm and Judge of the Manor of Wakefield Court, I am protected by the law.'

'The roads are not safe, Richard; this you know,' answered Wilhelmina. 'There are outlaws abroad.'

'If His Majesty commands me to go anywhere, I shall take Hubert and this.' He tapped the handle of the sword at his hip. 'Having Hubert at my side and my father's own weapon in my hand have always served me well and kept me safe.'

Lady Alecia nodded. 'We are sure that they have, yet we are also concerned about other matters beyond cutthroats and thieves.'

Richard raised an eyebrow. 'I am afraid I do not follow, Lady Alecia?'

'Malevolence, Richard. England is not safe because there are evil forces about in the land.'

'Evil forces, my lady?'

'Witchcraft, sorcery, necromancy, Richard. We hear of it every day.'

Wilhelmina squeezed his hand. 'We hear of it constantly from my father and from the servants.'

'It concerns us, Richard,' Lady Alecia went on. 'Which is why we want to give you something to protect you.' She reached for a casket on the table beside her chair, opened it and took out a metal medallion and chain. She handed it to Richard.

'It is heavy, Lady Alecia,' he said, hefting it in his palm before examining its surface upon which was engraved the figure of a saint carrying a child.

'It is an image of St Christopher, Richard,' Lady Alecia explained. 'The infant that he carries is our Lord, Jesus Christ. We ask St Christopher to protect you in all travels. And if you look on the other side, you will see the sign of the cross upon which our Lord was crucified. This was given to me when I was a young girl, and now I want you to have it. I had our priest bless it anew. It would please me, or rather please both Wilhelmina and I if you would wear it under your clothes.'

Richard immediately put it about his neck and dropped it under his shirt and tunic. As he adjusted his collar, he found himself thinking of Hubert and the arrowhead that he believed protected him from arrows and sudden death. It made him smile to think that he too would be wearing a charm to protect him. He did not, however, propose to tell Hubert about it.

'I thank you both, but now I cannot delay longer. The King awaits.'

Taking Lady Alecia's hand, he bowed and kissed it. Wilhelmina walked with him to the door. Once in the corridor, she hooked his arm with her own and dragged him after her to another room.

'Wilhelmina, I must —' he began, only to be silenced as she threw her arms about his neck and drew his head down to kiss him passionately.

'I have something else for you,' she said breathlessly once they parted. 'Something I could not give you in front of my mother.' She reached down and lifted the hem of her dress.

'Wilhelmina, no —!'

She placed a finger over his lips. 'Of course not, Richard, my love. Although you know that I long to have you ravage me in our marital bed.'

'It is only right that we wait until we are wed, my darling. I could not in good conscience rob you of your virginity. And if you are to have a child, it shall be in wedlock.'

She lifted her dress still higher until she revealed a scarlet silk garter. She untied it and pushed it into his hand. 'I want you to wear this on your leg. It will be our link, as I have its mate upon my other thigh. It will remind us both that once we are married, we can entangle our legs and join as husband and wife.'

Richard felt the blood rush to his cheeks as he felt desire for his fiancée almost overcome him. He suppressed his feelings and helped her to pull her gown down to cover her shapely limbs again. He stuffed her garter into his purse.

'I will wear it and think of you, my love. Now I must attend on His Majesty. I shall call to let you know whatever it is he wishes of me. I thank Lady Alecia and you for the medallion, but this garter I shall enjoy wearing so much more! Especially with the image that you have conjured up for me.'

Richard crossed the bailey courtyard towards the Great Hall. Two of the King's guards stood waiting on either side of the small stone staircase that led to an upper porch supported on an ornate octagonal column. Above the door was a large, rather splendid sundial that indicated that it was approaching three o'clock. As he mounted the steps, one of the guards turned and knocked on the door, which was opened by one of the castle's servants. He immediately bowed then led the way into a semi-circular oriel gallery and through this into a Presence Chamber, the walls of which were covered in pikestaffs, swords and banners. He waited at another huge door that led into the Great Hall, and when Richard reached the threshold, the servant pushed open the door, entered and announced in a loud voice: 'Sir Richard Lee, Your Majesty and my lords.'

There were three men standing talking over a map on the great table at the far end of the hall. Two were tall and the third was below average height and of stocky build with a salt-and-pepper beard. This was Sir Thomas Deyville, the Steward of Sandal Castle. He was wearing a knee-length purple robe and his usual beaver hat. He seemed to be perspiring and uneasy in the presence of King Edward the Second of Caernarvon. By contrast, resplendent in a blue tunic and hose, wearing a breastplate, with a light crown upon his head and with the distinctive three-forked beard that he cultivated, King Edward cut a dashing figure. On the other side of the table, Hugh le Despenser, the royal chamberlain and the King's favourite — an equally tall, dark-haired man of about Richard's age, somewhat gaudily dressed with a pill hat that barely covered his cascading locks — was jabbing a finger at the map and looked angry. They all looked round as Richard stepped in and bowed to the King.

'An honour to see you again, my liege.' Then to Hugh le Despenser and Sir Thomas he gave a half bow.

The King looked troubled, but at sight of the Sergeant-at-Law he smiled and gestured for him to approach. 'Sir Richard, I thank you for attending so promptly. We were just looking at the map of our Northern Realm to see the extent of the problem in hand.'

'The Manor of Wakefield is relatively trouble-free, Your Majesty,' Sir Thomas volunteered. 'I have worked hard on this over the years. Is this not so, Sir Richard?'

It was clear to Richard that his future father-in-law was appealing to him to be positive about his stewardship of the land under his control, although they both knew that until Richard had been appointed Sir Thomas had been harsh and overzealous.

'Sir Thomas is correct, Your Majesty. We dispense fair justice in the Manor Courts.'

The King eyed him knowingly, for it was because of Sir Thomas's reputation that he had appointed Sir Richard. At length, he nodded. 'Of this I know, Richard. And it is for that reason that I sent for you. I am pleased to hear that the Manor of Wakefield is relatively unblighted, unlike the neighbouring demesne of Pontefract.'

Hugh le Despenser slapped the table with the flat of his hand. 'Pontefract is a cesspit, Edward. This Lancaster nonsense has to be stopped. As must talk of these curses and these wretched pilgrims and their damnable beliefs.'

The King placed a hand on le Despenser's shoulder and nodded reassuringly, like a kindly parent comforting a youngster. 'It will all be stopped, Hugh, never fear. Let us talk calmly.'

The King's Eye clicked his tongue petulantly and slumped down in a chair. 'As Your Majesty desires.' Then with a feigned beatific smile, he waved both hands at his own face. 'Look, I am calmness personified.'

The King signalled for Richard to look at the map. 'See how clever William our great Conqueror was to have gifted his faithful followers with lands, yet dovetailed them together so that they are like hands with fingers interlaced. He did that to make each lord mutually dependent upon the neighbour and both dependent upon the throne. See how neighbouring towns can have different lords, Sir Richard?'

'I see and am aware of it, Your Majesty.'

'And yet I am not sure that it is not a problem in itself, for it can allow a pestilence to spread from finger to finger.'

Both Richard and Sir Thomas looked puzzled. 'I do not follow, Your Majesty,' Richard said. 'As far as I am aware, there is no pestilence spreading about the land.'

King Edward allowed himself a thin smile. 'I meant not an illness of the body, but a spiritual pestilence. Like this damnable cult that is growing around the traitor, Lancaster.'

Richard found himself thinking of the pilgrim, Timothy of Halifax, who he had seen that very morning. He chose not to mention it until he found out exactly why he had been summoned.

'You fought under the traitor Harclay, did you not, Sir Richard?' Hugh le Despenser asked, leaning languidly back in his chair.

'I did, my lord. When I served under him, I thought he was an able general and a fearless warrior.'

'And yet a traitor!' le Despenser said, leaning forward and slapping the map again.

'A traitor, indeed,' Sir Thomas agreed with alacrity.

'I wait to hear you say it, Sir Richard,' le Despenser persisted. 'The whole country is aware that he was stripped of his honours and titles for negotiating with Robert the Bruce without royal permission.'

Hugh le Despenser opened his mouth to speak again, but was cut short when King Edward raised his hand. 'No, Hugh, traitor though he was, even I have to admit that he won the Battle of Boroughbridge for us and in doing so captured my cousin, Thomas of Lancaster. For that I made him Earl of Carlisle. And then he betrayed me, as Sir Richard just said.'

He turned to Richard and the humour disappeared from his face. 'He had a fair trial, with Sir Geoffrey le Scrope, the Chief Justice of the King's Bench presiding, along with my own half-brother Edmund of Woodstock, the Earl of Kent, Lord John Hastings and three of my good and loyal knights, Sir John Pecche, Sir Ralph Basset and Sir John Wisham. He was found guilty of treason, the sentence for which under the law is —?' He stopped, looking expectantly at Richard.

'Death by being hanged, drawn and quartered, Your Majesty.'

'Exactly. But what happened after that?'

Richard frowned. 'His head was taken to you, Your Majesty, and then I believe it was sent to London, while his other —'

King Edward thumped his fist into his other palm and when he next spoke it was with obvious irritation in his voice. 'No, not that. I meant that instead of the country declaring that justice had been done by me, his king whom he had betrayed, rumours of this damnable curse he made before he was executed have grown rife.'

'He cursed His Majesty, myself and others, as well as cursing Lancaster,' said Hugh le Despenser, his voice trembling, though Richard could not tell whether it was from anger or fear.

King Edward clicked his tongue. 'Talk about the two curses has spread around the country. You have heard of them, of course? And so doubtless you also heard of this cult of St Thomas?'

Hugh le Despenser leaned forward and jabbed his finger at the map. 'Right here! Where we had that other traitor executed, they are using his tomb as a shrine. All manner of fools are declaring that miracles happen.'

Once again, Richard decided it was not an appropriate time to mention his case in court that morning. Instead, he said, 'I believe that pilgrims pass through Wakefield from the west to seek healing in Pontefract.'

King Edward grunted angrily. 'And that is treason against me, Sir Richard. I feel surrounded by evil, by malign forces being directed against me.'

Hugh le Despenser stood and poured wine into two goblets. 'There are those who seek to take the life of His Majesty and myself by necromancy and sorcery.'

Sir Thomas made the sign of the cross over his heart at the news. Richard merely raised an eyebrow. He was not himself given to believe in such things.

The King took the goblet offered to him by Hugh le Despenser and took a hefty swig. 'My chamberlain here speaks the truth, Sir Richard. My agents have uncovered such a plot using a necromancer in Coventry. And this is why I have sent for you. There have been several deaths in Carlisle and in Pontefract. The rumours are that they were linked to the curse by Thomas of Lancaster, but I do not choose to accept that. I believe that they may have been murders, perhaps using sorcery.'

Richard considered for a moment. 'Ah, then it is debatable whether it should be a matter for the Church courts to investigate, Your Majesty? Charges of witchcraft, divination and sorcery are usually considered under ecclesiastical law.'

King Edward nodded. 'Sorcery and witchcraft are Church court matters, that is true. Indeed, last month I instructed Archbishop Melton to crack down on the idolatry and worshiping that goes on in Pontefract, just as in June I commanded Steven de Gravesend, the Bishop of London, to stop people leaving offerings to the traitor Lancaster in St Paul's Cathedral. But still they came, even though I expressly told him it was a dangerous thing for him, for me the King and for the very souls of those poor benighted people who call him a saint.'

Hugh le Despenser snorted with indignation and slumped into his seat as the King went on.

'In July I ordered the removal of a tablet bearing the image of Lancaster from St Paul's, although I was unable to find out who had placed it there in the first place.' He took more wine. 'You can imagine the rumours that began. Some said that it had mystically appeared. Pah!'

Richard raised his hands. 'Surely mere superstition, Your Majesty?'

'Perhaps, but the damage it can do is immense. It foments feeling against me, against us. Did you hear about the latest outrage? I ordered Sir Clifford de Mosley, the Constable of Pontefract Castle, to go to the tomb in St John's Priory and stop it being used as a place of pilgrimage. He was pulled from his horse and two of his men were killed, beaten by a mob. Clifford de Mosley himself was ill in bed with a head wound for a full week, and his broken leg is still not recovered. I then sent Sir Henry le Scrope, my Chief Justice, to carry out a full investigation, but the useless oaf found nothing, arrested no one and achieved less than naught.'

Despenser harrumphed. 'He is Chief Justice no longer, of course. We are considering giving the appointment to his younger brother, Sir Geoffrey le Scrope, again.'

'Sir Geoffrey conducted the trial against Sir Andrew Harclay, did he not, Your Majesty?' Richard asked.

'He did, but then he fell ill with an ague that nearly killed him, so I gave Sir Henry the post. Now that he is recovered, I may elevate him again or give it to Hervey de Staunton.'

'I know Hervey de Staunton, Your Majesty. He is an able lawyer and would be a good Chief Justice.'

'But of course, the rumour-mongers said that Sir Geoffrey's illness was either a curse from Harclay, or part of the curse upon Harclay from Lancaster. This nonsense spreads like a canker. Carlisle, Pontefract and now Coventry. So what say you about this, Sir Richard Lee?'

Richard had noticed the King's temper slowly rising and how a thin patina of perspiration had formed on his brow. It was clear that both the King and his chamberlain were extremely worried about the so-called curse and the whole question about sorcery.

'I have heard of the Coventry case, Your Majesty,' Richard said, knowing that the King and his chamberlain had brought him here for a specific purpose yet to be explained. 'I know that those accused — a necromancer known as John of Nottingham, his assistant and twenty-three burghers of the town of Coventry — are to be tried by the King's Bench in London. A man, Richard de Sowe, is said to have died, possibly killed by sorcery. That would make it a felony, which falls under English Law, as it should do.'

'So you think that if murder has been done by sorcery, that is a felony?'

Richard bowed. 'Indeed, sire, murder is a felony. The difficulty may be in proving that sorcery was the cause. You would have to have strong evidence that sorcery was being practised and with a specific purpose.'

King Edward snorted. 'I need this whole issue of necromancy, sorcery, call it what you will, to be exposed for the malign thing that it is. The curses by the traitors Lancaster and Harclay, that the whole of England seems to know about, and now the use of sorcery to commit murder, they have to be shown as the work of the devil, directed against England's anointed King. You say that sorcery as the cause would have to be proven; well, that is why I have come here to Sandal to see you, Sir Richard, because there is a death in Pontefract that I am sure could only have come about through sorcery.'

'You believe a death to be suspicious, sire? If so, that is cause enough that it should indeed be investigated by the coroner.'

'And so it was. Sir Nigel Fairfax held an inquest, as he was bound to do, with a jury of twelve, all men who knew the deceased and were able to give evidence. He concluded that it was *felo de se* — self-murder.'

'But you do not agree, Your Majesty?'

'I do not. And I believe that these curses and the way that Pontefract has become a place of pilgrimage to a traitor who uttered a curse against me is all part of a diabolic threat to Christianity and to the very soul of England itself. The attacks on the Constable of Pontefract and the murders of his two servants is the result of that diabolic and demonic influence.'

Sir Thomas had barely said a word, but he now coughed to draw the King's attention. 'I think, Your Majesty, that there is no better man for this task than my future son-in-law. He has a unique understanding of justice and the law.'

King Edward smiled. 'Exactly what I feel, Sir Thomas. I knew that I would get wise counsel if I came to Sandal. And this is why I need a man I can trust, who has shown himself loyal and shrewd before, to go to Pontefract and investigate these matters and this suspicious death. I have not yet appointed a Chief Justice, and so in the interim I give you, Sir Richard Lee, full authority as my Circuit Judge of my Northern Realm to stay at Pontefract Castle and use however many men you need from the garrison.' He lifted the map and from under it picked up a warrant with the royal seal upon it. 'Here is your authority. But then again, you may choose not to have too heavy a presence with men at arms, as did Sir Henry.'

Richard accepted the warrant from King Edward. 'Can you tell me more of this suspicious death, Your Majesty?'

'Of course. It is of a man who has served me well. He was said to have suffered with melancholy so great that he hanged himself. But knowing the man as I do, I do not believe it. I think sorcery is the answer. He must have been bewitched.'

'And who is this person, Your Majesty?'

'His name is Perkin Cratwell. The royal executioner.'

CHAPTER FOUR

York

Simon of Holderness sat on the bench outside the dean's office in St Salvator's Hall, the imposing two-storeyed half-timbered building on Stonegate in the shadows of the Minster, idly squeezing a crop of blackheads and pimples around his nose. He counted himself a lucky fellow in all things except his skin, which defied healing with whatever concoction of quicksilver or brimstone, salve of boracic or unguent of lead or tartar that he procured from the apothecary. Although some counted him somewhat flabby in build and saggy about the jowls, he preferred to think of himself as being stout of both heart and body with a lust for life and the pleasures of the flesh.

He tugged at his wispy beard, which though never bushy he took pride in letting grow to a length of some six inches. And while he knew that few women would consider him good-looking, he cared not a whit, for he was often able to persuade or cajole many into lying with him, or at least parting their legs against a tree or wall while he took his pleasure of them.

As a summoner, or apparitor as the dean and those above him liked to term his position, he had more power than his old father, Grim the Fuller ever had. Of course, old Grim had wanted all nine of his sons to follow in his footsteps and become fullers like him and his father before him. That always made Simon laugh, because Grim walked his feet off throughout his life. He'd walked forty or fifty miles a day over in the East Riding without moving more than a few yards.

Literally by treading wool in great vats of stale urine he just walked back and forth without going anywhere. No, Simon had escaped and become a summoner's messenger and then a summoner himself back in Holderness. And as his master, Walter Lydford, had elevated himself, moving from one Ecclesiastical Court to another bigger one, Simon had enjoyed his rise in station, for with each move Walter Lydford had taken Simon with him.

'Simon Thorner of Holderness is the finest apparitor in Yorkshire,' Walter Lydford had told his superior, Cardinal Peter de Prés, the Archdeacon of York. 'He never fails to discharge a writ, and at seeking out wrongdoers and those guilty of moral turpitude, he has no equal. He is a veritable crusader against evil and the ways of the fallen.'

It was true, Simon knew. He had served more summonses from whichever Ecclesiastical Court he was employed by than any of the other summoners. Whether it be wretches who failed to attend church, drunkards, lewd women, adulterers or delinquent clergy suspected of usury, simony or parsimony, he summoned them *per apparitorem consistorii*. All who sinned against the Church and against God could be arrested and dragged before the Consistory Courts by the summoners to be judged and sentenced accordingly. And the dean gave Simon Thorner a free hand in identifying such cases.

Simon popped a pimple and wiped the white pus on the back of the bench as he wondered what the day would bring, what delightful cases the dean would send him on. He grinned to himself as he thought of what profit there would be in it for him, whether to eat, drink wine or ale, fill his purse or ease the pressure and desire he always felt within his codpiece with fornication. And he could do it all in the name of the Lord and with the full backing of the Ecclesiastical Court. He just had to ensure that no one ever found him out.

A handbell clanged from the dean's office and he rose with alacrity, knocked upon the stout metal-studded door and let himself in upon hearing the dean's call of 'Come!'

Walter Lydford, Dean of St Salvator's Church and Commissary General of the York Consistory Court, was sitting behind a large desk strewn with documents, clearly in a pensive mood. Dressed in his long black gown adorned only by a plain silver crucifix hanging from his neck, and with his hooked nose, black tonsured hair and habitual stoop, he fitted the nickname of Father Raven that he was called behind his back by the summoners and court clerks. In his hand was a black feather quill, which he had just dipped into an inkwell and was holding above a document. After a momentary reflective hesitation, he signed his name, the noise of the quill tip scratching on the parchment echoing authoritatively in the great oak-panelled hall. Indeed, as Simon knew only too well, the dean's signature could destroy a man as surely as an arrow in his back. The latter would be quick, but a writ of excommunication could make a man or woman an outcast from the church, the parish, indeed from the whole of Christendom. It was a condemnation to eternal damnation.

The dean's clerk, the aged Bartholomew Ditch, dressed in a plain brown gown, sat at a smaller table in a corner of the great office. A candle guttered upon his neat, ordered table, testifying to the fact that he had just melted the end of a wax stick and stamped an official seal on the bottom of a writ of summons in front of him.

'Simon, come and sit,' the dean ordered, raising his dark eyes to gaze upon the summoner as he placed his quill upon the desk and gestured to the low stool. 'You are going to be busy these next few days with these summonses, and I want you to know precisely why, because your tasks are of the utmost importance.'

Simon Thorner bowed and sat as he was bidden. 'It will be my honour to serve as always, my lord. Where will I be going?'

'To Pontefract again, on most important business. The Archdeacon, Cardinal Peter de Prés, is, as you know, abroad at this time in Santa Pudenziana in Rome, so I act in his name.' He touched the cross upon his chest and closed his eyes momentarily, as if making a silent blessing. 'Archbishop Melton himself has ordered the Archdeacon's court to issue these summonses and deal with this tide of irreligion and blasphemy that continues to blight the town of Pontefract.'

Simon made the sign of the cross over his heart. 'Is it to do with the tomb of Thomas of Lancaster again, Your Grace?'

Eight times in the past few months he had been sent on the journey to Pontefract to summons people of all walks of life before the York Consistory Court. It was a journey that was often arduous if the weather was inclement, and not without danger on the road, especially when he passed through forests where outlaws might lie in wait. But he enjoyed his sojourns around Pontefract.

'It is indeed. There are eight writs here for idolatry and damage to church property in a riot. A mob attacked the Constable of Pontefract and his men when they tried to disperse a crowd attempting to force their way in to the Priory of St John. The constable was pulled from his horse and injured, and two of his men were killed.'

Simon looked startled. 'I had heard something of this, Your Grace, but is it not a matter for the secular courts?'

Father Raven nodded. 'It is, and it was investigated by order of the King, but not a single person was charged with the

67

attacks. Yet that is not our concern; these eight individuals were recognised and have been deposed by honest and good citizens as having damaged the doors of the priory. That means they insulted the Church, so they must be summoned to the Consistory Court. We cannot permit such outrages.'

Simon bowed. 'Of course not, Your Grace. I shall find these people and summons them.'

'And you may deputise local men as you see fit.'

'I know several stout fellows who were once fighting men that I may call upon,' Simon volunteered.

The dean cleared his throat. 'There have been more false accounts of miracles, and now a wretched girl by the name of Jane Henshaw has claimed to have seen a vision of Lancaster the traitor surrounded by divine light. We cannot allow this, for it is all just the devil's mischief-making.'

Simon nodded with a deep frown of annoyance on his face. He knew it was politic to align himself with the views of the dean. In truth, it mattered not a whit to him what the summons was about as long as it afforded him no harm, and permitted him to sate one or other of his many lusts.

'You will summon this shameless girl so that I can examine her in court. If you can find whoever put her up to making such a story up, then they must be summoned and also arrested under my authority.' He placed the writ for the girl upon the eight others. 'Now these next writs are extremely serious. I have had reports that some of the Black Monks at St John's Priory, wherein the tomb of Thomas of Lancaster is contained, are selling relics, blood-soaked soil from the traitor's execution, which means they are selling property that belongs to the Church. That is the sin of simony.'

He slapped the edge of the table, making the inkpot shake. 'In addition, purporting that these so-called things that they sell in pots and jars are somehow blessed relics is the greater sin of blasphemy, because Lancaster is not a saint, nor even one who has been canonised. So, Simon of Holderness, these cases are of extreme importance and it will probably take you time to search out the individuals and deliver the summonses. I have left several blank summonses for you to fill in their names, when you discover them. And, of course, I rely upon you to keep your eyes and ears open for other cases of dissolute behaviour.'

Simon nodded. 'I regard every case that you give me as of the utmost importance, as they are all in the Lord's name.' In truth, he cared little about the veracity of the cases he was given to summon to court, since he had almost no genuine belief in God or angels or saints. If anything, he saw personal merit in enjoying the sins of the flesh and in mammon and the power of his position. 'So, is there a time limit, Your Grace, for my previous visits to Pontefract have shown me that there is much evil and corruption abroad? Even upon pilgrimages — as I know from my own experience last year, when I joined a party of pilgrims travelling from London to the tomb of the true St Thomas Becket at Canterbury — there were some among us who were less pious than others.'

The dean's lips almost formed a smile. Simon knew the sort of things to say to please him. Simon was himself an ambitious man, and he recognised the trait in others, even those of the loftiest station. 'The next Archdeacon's Court is in ten days,' the dean replied. 'You have until then to issue the summonses and arrange that these miscreants and sinners attend here on that day. The girl in particular must attend.'

'Then I had better make haste, for it will take me a day to travel there and a day back, Your Grace.'

The dean snapped his fingers at the clerk. 'Bartholomew, gather the writs together and arrange for the kitchens to have food and a flagon of ale made ready for Simon Thorner.'

As the aged clerk rose, bowed and shuffled out the door, Walter Lydford rose and pointed to the altar at the other end of the room. 'We shall say a prayer together to keep you safe when you are among sinners, Simon.'

Simon gave a half smile and bowed his head as he rose to his feet. 'I thank you, Your Grace. I am always grateful for the Lord's protection.'

The smile broadened as he followed the dean to the altar. He was also pleased to have the protection of his short sword, his cudgel and the bollock dagger he kept in easy reach down the side of his right riding boot.

The old grey pony had served Simon of Holderness well over many years, and he held the beast in some affection. Indeed, he thought more of it than he did about most people, which may have been why he called it Jethro, after his youngest brother, and always made sure that he had plenty of carrots in the sack that hung from the pommel of his saddle. It bore him on the journey from York to Wetherby and thence south along the Great North Road that ran all the way down from the troubled borders with Scotland to far-off London, passing as it did through Aberford and a number of villages and hamlets on the way to Pontefract. All manner of folk travelled on it: wagons, packhorse trains, troops of pilgrims and even shepherds moving their flocks to market. It was hard going, especially when it rained as it was likely to do at this time of year.

Along the way he had stopped at the village of Micklefield, where he tethered Jethro and allowed him to graze on the village pasture before he went inside the modest inn and ordered bread and cheese and a mug of ale.

A familiar customer now, he was greeted with a grin by Judkin, the landlord. 'You are on your way to Pontefract again, Master Simon?' Judkin asked, raising his voice just enough to ensure that the dozen or so drinkers could hear.

Simon knew that it was a subtle warning to the customers and noticed the shuffling of feet and the surreptitious glances in his direction. He nodded and graced him with one of his most benign smiles as he took a seat at a vacant table. 'Sadly, my work is never done, sir. There is so much evil about that the dean, my master at the Church Court, will have me wandering back and forth along this road until either my pony Jethro keels over or I myself fall from his saddle into the dust. Who will mourn for me, I wonder?'

The innkeeper placed a mug of his best ale in front of Simon and clapped his hands. 'Bread and cheese and a good apple for Master Simon the summoner here,' he said to the old woman who put her head round the doorframe at his clap. Turning to Simon with a tremulous smile, he continued, 'You won't find any trouble around here, sir. We are all Godfearing folk who go to church without fail and mind our own business.'

A surly-looking fellow hunched over his mug mumbled sourly, 'Aye, we know it's best to mind our places.'

'How so, friend?' Simon asked, raising his voice. 'You good people have nothing to fear from me.'

'Didn't say I was afeared of you, summoner,' the man replied, half-turning his head. 'I said it's best to mind our place. That's what I do, no matter what I sees or hears.'

He was surrounded by three or four other roughly dressed men, all clearly workers on the land. One of them prodded him. 'Why don't you heed your own words, Will Brooker?'

The old woman appeared and deferentially shoved a wooden bowl containing a hunk of cheese, a large piece of bread and a neatly polished apple in front of Simon. Simon thanked her and immediately stowed the apple in his sleeve. 'I will share this with my pony later, Mistress,' he said, favouring her with a smile and being rewarded with a toothless grin as she backed away. 'It sounds as if our friend here has things that he sees and hears that trouble him,' he suggested softly to Judkin the innkeeper.

'Will Brooker has had a mug or two too many, I fear, sir.'

'I can speak for myself,' the labourer said loudly, without turning. 'Maybe it's time that folk know about a certain priest that keeps preaching at us and shoving that collecting bowl of his at us every service. Not just wanting money, neither. There's favours and there's favours, but I don't hold with who he asks.'

Simon smiled inwardly. Here was a titbit that sounded worthy of following up. There could be profit in it for him, when he made his way back towards York, if he had time to investigate this priest, who seemed overzealous in collecting money for his church and certain favours for himself. It sounded like licentiousness, a good enough reason to be served a summons to the Church Court. He took a gulp of his ale then reached for his purse. It would be worth the cost of a few mugs to put these folk at their ease before he returned in a few days.

'Let these fine fellows all have another ale,' he said to Judkin. Then he added in a whisper, 'When I come back in a few days, I would like to speak with Will Brooker over there. You can arrange that, can't you?'

An anxious look passed over the innkeeper's face, but it was quickly replaced by a knowing smile as Simon counted out a number of coins on the table and shoved them towards him with his thumb.

'If he isn't here when you visit again, I'll send a boy to fetch him, sir.'

Simon nodded as the innkeeper scooped up his money and went to serve ale. He pulled out his knife and wiped the blade on his sleeve before cutting his cheese. The day was looking good, with promise of reward for him one way or another. Either he'd catch this wrongdoing priest and serve a summons on him or he'd frighten the life from him with the threat of a summons and lighten him of whatever money he had inveigled out of these simple villagers. Either way, it would put him in a good light with the villagers, for the priest would like as not change his behaviour. Simon liked it when he could do a good turn to somebody and still profit by it.

As he approached Pontefract the terrain became gently undulating, intermittently wooded or cultivated in the characteristic strip farming of the area. Large fields were divided into strips or selions, measuring about thirty feet in breadth by a furlong in length. Each of these were divided up by green unploughed balks for the serfs to walk upon and lead their oxen, as indeed several were doing as he passed.

And when he passed through the open downlands everywhere he saw the presence of sheep as they nibbled the grass, or were being shepherded in flocks with tinkling bells. Great barns of stone and timber were stacked with fleeces, and the closer he got to Pontefract he saw packhorses and wagons laden with wool on their way to the market.

Whenever Simon saw the back-breaking work that folk had to endure to put meagre rations on the table for their families, he thanked the Lord that he had been given wit to enjoy the many comforts of life.

'There is an apple in my sleeve all for you, Jethro,' he said, patting the pony's neck as they began the ascent of the ridge on top of which lay the town of two thousand souls that was Pontefract. First they came upon the town's ditch, causing him to cover his nose as they passed across it with its stench of offal, dung and putrefying rubbish, then through the large north gate, guarded by a couple of bored-looking watchmen. Ahead of him upon the huge rocky mound rose the mighty honey-coloured Pontefract Castle with its seven towers, battlemented walls and its magnificent keep.

Simon was now well accustomed to the geography of the town and the surrounding area, having made it his business to know where all of the religious establishments were located, for it was often there that he was sent or where he sniffed out immorality. Such cases were always of far more interest to his boss the dean than the lesser transgressions of the lower orders.

The great Cluniac Priory of St John the Evangelist was on the high ground to the north-east of the borough. It was home to twenty or so of the Black Monks, so called because of the black habits of their order. He knew that most of the monks were French, having come from their parent abbey *La Charité-sur-Loire*, and that they considered themselves under its authority rather than that of the law of the land or of the Church.

Near to it was the old Saxon St Nicholas's Hospital, where the monks had first lived when they'd built the priory a century before, but which now cared for pilgrims and the infirm. Further south and some distance from the centre of the town stood St Mary Magdalene's Hospital, built near a Lazar House, which had originally been established by the Order of St Lazarus of Jerusalem, or the Leper Brothers of Jerusalem, for the care of lepers and those suffering from contagious diseases. To the west of the castle, in a valley not far from the town marketplace near to where several roads met, stood the Friary of St Richard, home to about fifteen mendicant Dominican friars.

Of all these, it was the Black Monks of St John's Priory, the monks of the Cluniac order, that Simon had been directed to investigate and to deliver some of the writs that Walter Lydford had said were of especial importance.

But he was not yet concerned about his work for the dean. His own comfort and that of Jethro came first. He turned onto the Micklegate, one of the three main roads in the town, which led from the low ground below the castle up the hill to the centre of the town. Urging Jethro through the crowds of pilgrims, labourers, goatherds and shepherds moving their animals towards the Westcheap market, he made his way to the Fleshbooths where the butchers plied their trade, then onto Skinner's Lane at the end of which was the Pikestaff Inn, the hostelry with an old blunt pikestaff nailed to its wall above the door lintel. He always stayed there on his visits as he judged it a good base. Importantly, Harald Barrowman the landlord was both discreet and a good source of information about things going on in the town.

Having stabled Jethro, he took his belongings into the hostelry and lay down to sleep for an hour or two in the curtained-off cubicle that had been allocated to him in the large partitioned room above stairs reserved for paying guests. Somewhat refreshed by sleep and with his appetite healthily stoked up, he ate a meal of the bread and perpetual stew that

Harald's wife managed to make half palatable by adding onions and garlic aplenty. Just the way he liked it.

Darkness had fallen when he dressed in a nondescript hood and cloak and let himself out into the Pontefract street, transformed now from that of a working town into a place where those seeking entertainments took to the alleys and backstreets. Many like him did so clandestinely and dressed accordingly. All either made their way to whatever source of entertainment they were after before the curfew at either the eight or the nine o'clock bell, or they ensconced themselves somewhere until cockcrow the next morning. Those who were willing to disobey the curfew, which included Simon of Holderness, who regarded his position as immunity against such restrictions, were usually adept at merging into the shadows to avoid the night watch and the gong wagons. The former could be an inconvenience, while the latter shovelled and stirred up odours that were best avoided.

Nonetheless, hanging from his belt he kept a small lantern that he could display if he was ever challenged, to show that he was a good upstanding citizen and that it was just that his lantern would not light.

He stood at the corner of one of the backstreets behind Salter's Row, the street of the salt and spice merchants, watching the bawdy house until the street was clear enough for him to cross and knock upon its heavy door with the prearranged knock that Bardolph, the owner of the establishment, had told him to use. Although they were never bothered by the town's watch, since he paid handsomely not to be bothered, there was no sense in tempting providence and letting in a troublemaker. Bardolph had made up umpteen little rap-a-tap ditties, each of which identified a particular customer.

A grille in the door slid open, and Bardolph himself peered out from the dimly lit interior. 'I thought it wouldn't be too long before you paid us another visit, master,' he said as he unbolted the door and let Simon of Holderness inside.

'I can't let an opportunity to visit with my old friend pass by,' he returned, throwing back his hood.

'Then you'll drink some mead with me first before I call one of the wenches. Which one shall it be this time? And, of course, there is no charge for you, sir.'

The summoner chuckled and patted the brothelkeeper on the back. 'I'll take Gertrude, the noisy one. I have it in mind to make some noise myself,' he said suggestively.

Bardolph cackled as if he had just heard the finest joke and led the way through to his counting room, as he liked to call it, where he proffered a seat to Simon next to the guttering candle while he pulled out the stopper of a flask of mead.

'You are a good friend, Bardolph. I drink to your health.'

'Aye, and I to yours. I fancy that your skin is faring better with some medicine. Is it from one of our apothecaries?'

Simon laughed and clinked his goblet against his host's. 'Mayhap it burns a little less, but spots, wens and skin blackworms I have had all of my life. It is a good thing that I have other talents that don't frighten wenches away.'

They drank and shared some dried meat and chopped onions.

'So has our noisy Gertrude much news to be noisy about with me?' Simon asked, raising an eyebrow.

Again Bardolph laughed. 'Oh, I'm sure she does, master. Make it worth her while with a few coins and your usual promise and she'll tell you all of the little secrets she worms out of her customers when she's working her magic on them.' He winked knowingly. 'I'll have her bring a flask of mead, too.'

Simon chuckled. Bardolph and his wenches had given him many valuable tips that had led to either writs or bribes for him. In return, he gave them his protection. The freedom from being summoned to the Church Courts and the penalties that could bring to women of the bawdy house made them all eager to please Simon of Holderness, despite his flaking skin, onion breath and overall evil smell of brimstone or lead or whatever unguent he spread over his face and chest.

An hour later, Simon and Gertrude rolled apart on the large creaking pallet bed, both naked as the day they were born and lathered in perspiration. They had coupled four times and in between each vigorous and noisy flesh-smacking session they drank mead, some of which he dribbled over her ample breasts and licked and sucked off while she giggled and wriggled and whispered secrets about her customers to him.

He discovered that an ostler of the town had been boasting about how big his manhood was, as if she didn't already know from experience, and of how he had a partiality for certain ponies.

'I will call on this fellow,' Simon had said with a guffaw as he tugged at his wispy beard before licking mead from his fingers. 'I'll warn him never to try anything with my Jethro unless he wants to find himself gelded by a hoof. That is before I summons him to court for bestial depravity.'

Gertrude shrieked with laughter, a different noise entirely from her shrill gasping and laughing when they coupled.

Two other minor peccadillos were recounted to him, which he thought he probably would not bother with, unless he needed to make up his summoning numbers. Yet her last tasty morsel, which he knew she had kept back, really interested him.

'There is a man who has come to me several times these past few weeks. A strapping, clean-shaven fellow, who calls himself a leather merchant. He is not one of our own here in Pontefract, but from over west, judging by his accent, though he tries to disguise it. I am sure you will find him about the town.'

'And you can tell accents, can't you, my girl?' Simon said, squeezing her rump firmly.

She laughed. 'That I can. He likes to hurt a bit, to smack my bum before he does it. You like to squeeze, but he likes it when he makes me sore so that I squeal like a pig. I should charge him extra for that, if I only dared.'

'And what is it about him that I should know?' Simon took more mead then began gently stroking her breasts.

'See, that's the difference between you two. He likes to bite or pinch them. And unlike you he takes no clothes off, apart from his breeches. He even keeps his gugel hood on.'

'A shy fellow, then?'

'No, not shy, but one who has a secret.'

'Go on.'

'I didn't dare pull back his gugel, but while he was in the throes of his pleasure I slid a hand inside his hood and stroked his head. He had a tonsure. It was recently done and not stubbly.'

'Could he have been balding?'

'No, it was shaven. A monk or a friar, I thought at first. But then, I am sure he is no monk! He is half stallion and always rampant when he comes. And he only ever wants me.'

'What did he look like, though?'

Gertrude giggled. 'I don't know. His gugel was always pulled low and the cord pulled to hood his face. He never kissed me on the lips. That wasn't the type of lovemaking he was after. I realised well enough that he wore that gugel to hide himself. Maybe he was disfigured? Maybe he was ashamed of something, I don't know. I knew not to push my luck.'

Simon chuckled, his interest piqued. If there was one thing he liked above all else it was finding out about a friar. He liked nothing better than confronting a sanctimonious and licentious friar and watching him writhe like a worm on a fishing hook. But if this man wasn't really a friar, why wear a gugel hood to conceal a tonsure he didn't need?

Either way, this fellow was guilty of something. He was a holy sort, either guilty of forbidden fornication or of apostasy, in that he was denying his cloth. The dean would want him summoning, for often he had told Simon that an apostate who has forsaken the Lord and renounced his benevolence must be brought to task or ejected into the wilderness.

Or what if he was one who sometimes pretended to be a friar? Why would he do that?

He would think about it later, after he'd satiated his needs and could think soberly.

In a house no more than a furlong away, four people were gathered round a table by the light of three black candles.

'How long before the incantations will work?' one of the men asked the oldest man, who was mumbling over three wax effigies on the table. They were all of a dusky colour, the result of having been made from tallow wax mixed with pig's blood. The old man was dressed in a black robe and was making passes in the air above one of the effigies, which was the length of a man's arm, fully clothed in fine silk and with a small crown on the head and a beard with three points.

'Don't talk to him while he casts,' the woman snapped. 'It could be dangerous and could ruin the spell.'

The old man suddenly laughed. 'Fear not, the magic is powerful and it will work, given time. Leave the casting to me; your tasks are to keep me protected.' He turned his attention to the effigy next to it, a similar sized figure also clad in silks. Again he made passes and spent some minutes muttering words that none of the others could understand.

'Will they burn John of Nottingham?' asked the man who had first spoken, in a hushed voice.

'It is possible,' whispered the woman. 'As they would burn the Master here.'

The old man finished his passes and looked up at the other three. 'My brother John of Nottingham will not die by fire. He will not allow it,' he said emphatically. He turned his attention to a smaller effigy, that of a young woman wearing a small smock with an apron over it. Once again, he started to make passes.

'What have you done with the headsman's doll?' asked the third man, who had not yet spoken.

'It is no longer needed here,' said the old man, whom the woman referred to as 'the Master.' He gave a cruel throaty laugh. 'It served its purpose well enough. We stretched its neck and now it lies in the graveyard box. It has no place now with these living dolls.'

'We will show it and the others as proof when it is all done,' the woman added. 'Then the whole land will know the truth and our just cause will prevail.'

The old man reached into a bag and drew out a bodkin with a wooden handle. He inserted the tip into the candle flame and held it there until it was red hot. Then he lowered it and shoved it into one eye of the effigy, so that it melted the wax, which ran over the face as if it was blood.

'And now the other,' he said, repeating the process on the other wax eye socket.

The third man gave a throaty laugh. '*If thine eye offends thee, pluck it out!* And so, it shall be just like this.' He turned to the woman. 'Have you prepared for your part?'

She put a hand on the other man's arm. 'We are ready.'

CHAPTER FIVE

Simon of Holderness planned to spend the next day wandering about the town talking to people to pick up the local news. He considered this important rather than straightaway searching out those individuals for whom he had writs already prepared, signed and sealed by the dean, since it always gave him an idea of the subjects that occupied the conversations of the common folk. Then when he did begin to track his targets, he did so by first of all identifying them and spying on them at a distance, circling them like a hawk before swooping on them when they were least likely to escape.

As he was already familiar to many people, an inevitable consequence of being a summoner, he had done his best to look more like a moderately successful tradesman. He applied a double helping of the salve of boracic to his face to at least conceal his pustules and pale the inflammation that normally gave him a ruddy complexion. A smearing of pig fat obtained from Mistress Barrowman's kitchen allowed him to slick his hair so that he could hang it behind his ears rather than letting it dangle like bunches of rat tails from under the shapeless hat he normally wore. The effect of this application upon his straggly beard, although he did not realise it, was to make it look uncommonly like the tail of a pig. With a blue doublet, his best leather boots and his writs in a satchel, he had first gone to check upon Jethro to ensure that the ostler had taken good care of him.

If the fellow is the rogue Gertrude mentioned and shows a limp or any sign that one of Jethro's hooves has smitten him, then I will issue him a writ for having unnatural carnality.

The thought made him laugh inwardly, yet he was relieved to find Jethro content in a stall with plenty of hay and an assurance from the ostler that he would receive ample feed. As he was leaving, he chided himself for not pressing Gertrude for better details about the ostler's physical features other than the size of his manhood. Going round the other stables without such knowledge could waste much of his time, so he determined that he would pay her another call before he continued the search for that particular sinner.

It somewhat startled him to find that much of the open talk around the town was about St Thomas, as he was now commonly being referred to. Whereas on his last visit he had often heard people talking about him in hushed tones, now there had been a noticeable increase in reverence for the executed earl's memory. It took only the slightest of prompts from him to get an opinion.

'He was a saint, no mistake about it,' a farrier told him.

'Martyred by them as are naught but sinners,' said an old maid on her way up the hill towards the castle, when Simon had picked up a log that she had dropped and asked where the earl had been executed. 'It is blessed ground now, with a cross upon it,' she replied.

'There ain't no doubt about it; just like our Lord, he's shown himself to that girl after he's been dead a year and more,' a pedlar told him when he stopped to buy two apples, one for him and one for Jethro. 'And she's a virgin, so she ain't no liar, is she?'

Simon had no such certainties either about the virtues of virginity or claims of still possessing it, but in his guise as a tradesman he smiled affably and agreed. But this was what he wanted to know about — the young girl that he had a writ for and whom Dean Walter Lydford was so anxious to question in court.

'So, who is this young virgin and what did she see?'

'She's the daughter of a girdler, sir. She saw St Thomas as clear as day, surrounded by holy light, so they say.'

'Have you talked to her yourself?'

The pedlar shook his head. 'Not I, and glad am I that I hasn't.'

Simon frowned. 'Why so?'

'Because seeing things we shouldn't see can be too much for poor folk like us. Maybe it was for her alone to see the saint.' Then suddenly less keen to talk and conscious that he was missing opportunities to sell his apples, he nodded and ambled off into the crowd, crying out about the value of his apples and their lack of worms.

A girdler's daughter? He felt he needed to find out more. Why would a saint reveal himself to a girdler's daughter? He walked down the Micklegate in the direction of the marketplace, where he was able to hear more about the girdler and his daughter and get directions to the girdler's shop.

He found out more, too. The story was told to him several times by different people, and it was always the same.

The girdler's name was Wilfred Henshaw, and his daughter Jane was fifteen. Henshaw's wife had died five years before and Jane helped him in his shop, stitching girdles and belts. On the Friday three weeks before, she had been delivering a basket of belts and other leatherwork to the guardhouse at the castle. For some reason, she had felt compelled to visit the Monk's Hill where the earl had been beheaded. As she approached it, she apparently felt overwhelming joy and suddenly a ball of light rose from the earth into the air, where it floated for a few moments like a miniature sun. She was dazzled and rubbed her eyes, but when she looked again a man dressed in white linen, bearded and with long hair and a benevolent smile, was standing in front of her. She immediately fell to her knees, trembling and fearful. She made the sign of the cross. Then he spoke to her and told her that he was Thomas, the earl whose life was taken on that spot. He told her to come closer, so that he could lay his hand upon her head and give her the gift of healing. She fell asleep and woke when darkness was starting to fall. A monk from St John's Priory found her there and took her home. Miraculously, he said that as soon as she had taken his arm, a painful twisted ankle suddenly felt well again. It was he who told Wilfred Henshaw as well as everyone that they passed on the way to her home. Inevitably, news spread all over Pontefract and people came in droves to the girdler's shop, asking to see if she could heal them.

'She cured my ear that had been pouring pus and blood,' a butcher told Simon in his guise as a tradesman.

'My agues have gone completely,' said a coney seller. 'She was given this gift by St Thomas.'

'She looks different herself,' said another. 'She's like a beautiful angel.'

Simon nodded each time he heard the story and feigned wonder at each retelling. He guessed that if the girdler had any sense he would be eyeing up all those who came to her for healing and marking out those that might make a good husband. He would likely not have to give a dowry, and if he could marry her well, he could profit himself.

But despite his naturally cynical nature, Simon wondered whether the girl actually *had* seen the executed earl and *had* been given the gift of healing by him. If so, then he would have the perfect test of her abilities, for the skin of his face had defied every single potion, concoction, unguent or salve. All they ever managed to do was to conceal his pustules and boils as he hoped they were doing at that moment.

It would be worth trying, he decided. If it worked, he'd even try to save her from the excommunication he was pretty sure the dean would have in mind for her.

The girdler's shop was a nondescript building like the row of other shops and businesses on Walkergate, a small street leading off to the south from Southgate, the lowest of the three streets leading from the castle to the market area of the town. It was the street of the cloth dressers, the drapers, the leather workers and the girdlers. They all tended to distinguish themselves from each other by hanging some picture of a tool or article they produced above or on the door of the establishment. Henshaw's shop had a faded depiction of a bodkin above the door. Apart from the girdler's, the shops seemed less busy than the vegetable, food and poultry booths that were dotted around the great Cross of St Oswald in the marketplace on the other side of Southgate. A small crowd was gathered around the door of the shop.

'Why is the girdler so busy?' Simon asked a man carrying a young child on the edge of the crowd.

'We're all waiting to see the healing girl,' the man returned. 'You'll need to wait your turn if it's her you've come for, too. And you'd better have coins to pay old Henshaw.'

Ah, thought the summoner. If the father was charging folk to see his daughter, then it began to sound like charlatanry. That would strengthen the case against her, which the dean would appreciate.

The young girl the man was carrying turned her head to look at Simon and immediately shied away and began to cry. It was a reaction that he was used to and knew that it was because of his face, despite his best efforts to cover the blemishes and boils with a salve. Suppressing an impulse to stick his tongue out at the child, he put on his most benevolent smile and moved sideward round the crowd.

He was debating with himself whether to wait and see the girl himself when ahead of him he saw a face that he recognised. It shocked him, and he rubbed his eyes to try to see better. And when he blinked and looked again, that shocked him even more.

Well, now, he thought, *here is a catch and no mistaking.*

He detached himself nonchalantly from the crowd, which had swelled even in the time since he had arrived. He walked further down the street and found an alley to step into. It afforded him cover in case he himself was recognised. This changed his plans dramatically, and he decided that the girl could wait. Now he had a far more important quarry to spy upon.

Simon thought the girdler's shop had probably never had so many people pass through its shabby door. There were all sorts of people — quality folk to ragged beggars, old women with sticks, lame men with bowed legs, some with eyepatches, others with skin ailments even worse than his own. He watched them shuffle in, throwing money into a big bowl held by a pasty-faced fellow that he assumed must be Henshaw the girdler himself. What happened then he did not see, for as soon as one or two came out there were others ready to go in.

They all seem happy, like they've seen an angel or something, he mused.

At last he saw the face he had recognised come out. The clothing was all different, as was the outward appearance, but seeing the face from the front, Simon had no doubt. And the person was not alone, which interested him.

Landing this one will be the making of me, he thought. *But I'll have to be careful, and I will need to hire some burly fellows and a wagon to get back to York.*

He knew it would please not only the dean, but those even higher than him.

An expert at following people without being detected, Simon found himself tracking up back alleys and side streets, clearly taking a circuitous route.

They don't know I'm following, of that I'm sure, he thought. *Yet they are avoiding the main streets. That means they would rather not be seen. Or mayhap they don't want any to know where they have been?*

At last they entered a house. Simon committed what it looked like to memory so that he would be able to spy on it at will. He smirked and absent-mindedly reached to rub a spot on his nose, inadvertently clearing some dried white salve from around it to expose the purple carbuncle that was forming beneath. *So, now I know where to find you*, he thought. *I'll at my leisure find out what you're doing in Pontefract. But now, to work.*

He retraced his steps back down the hill towards the marketplace. It was time for him to pay a visit to Jane the Healer, as she was now being described.

He was not aware that he was at that moment himself being spied upon. A figure was watching and following, but keeping to the shadows and alleyways to avoid alerting the summoner. This skilled hunter knew how to stalk unseen, so they could go in for the kill when the prey least expected it.

The crowd of eager sick and curious folk had thinned out, and Simon had little time to wait when he returned. Inside the shop the girdler was sitting on a stool by his workbench, with his wooden bowl beside him.

'Any donation you feel able to make,' he said. 'My daughter has no mother, and blessed St Thomas of Lancaster who was martyred upon the Monk's Hill chose to reveal himself to her in a vision and he gave her the gift of healing. Any favour for her will go to a good cause, and she will share with St Nicholas's Hospital, where her mother was looked after until she died.'

Clearly, he had prepared his little speech and had repeated it so often that it had become second nature and tripped off his tongue. And judging by the amount of money that had accumulated, it looked as if few girdles, belts and purses would need to be mended or made for some time.

'I am sorry to hear of your loss, sir,' said Simon, ostentatiously dropping a silver groat in the bowl. 'I have heard much of your daughter's skill and hope that she may alleviate this minor skin affliction of mine.'

Henshaw looked doubtfully at the summoner's face. 'You may go through the curtain to see Jane once the old dame comes out. But know you that she is not an apothecary or a leech. She will give you no ointment or elixir. She will simply give you the healing touch that St Thomas bestowed on her.'

'You say you are going to make a donation to St Nicholas's Hospital, sir?' Simon asked. 'Where is this place?'

'It is up beyond the castle, down the hill and up the rise towards St John's Priory. It is but a short walk from the castle.'

The curtain parted and an elderly woman and her son came out, smiling and full of hope. At a sign from Henshaw, Simon went through.

Jane the Healer was sitting on another stool in front of another workbench that was littered with piles of leather, belts, purses and all of the tools of the girdler's trade. There were bodkins, threads, cords, needles and various knives, shears and scissors.

She was a comely girl, Simon thought, wearing a plain wool kirtle over a shirt and a cap over what appeared to be blonde hair, judging by the stray wisps that protruded from it. She had an apron on top and was nibbling a small pastry of some sort.

'Excuse me, sir. I have not eaten a full meal today, and so many good folk have brought me such tempting morsels.'

'You have been busy, I will wager,' Simon said, pulling his hat from his head and pushing his hair back behind his ears. 'I am not from the town, but I hear that you have been blessed with the power to heal.'

'I have, sir. I know not why, but St Thomas chose to reveal himself to me upon the place where he lost his...' She hesitated for a moment, then cleared her throat with a little cough. 'Where he lost his life. What can I help you with, sir?'

He noticed that she had averted her eyes from his face and was looking at her hands, which were covered in calluses from all the stitching and sewing of leather that she did.

He touched his cheeks and then generally pointed at his face. 'It is my skin. My face and my chest have always been like this. Nothing the apothecary gives helps more than a bit. If you could heal me, I would be grateful until the day I die.' He was sure to emphasise how much he suffered, although in truth he was so used to it that it barely incommoded him at all, apart from when he wanted to lie with a woman.

'Could you come closer, sir, and kneel down. I have no skill in physic myself, I just trust in the healing touch that St Thomas gave me when he touched my head.'

Simon dropped to one knee before her and smiled benignly as she lay her hands over his face and then over his head. As she did, she mumbled a prayer. 'Would you like to heal my chest, too? Shall I bare it for you?'

She raised her hands swiftly. 'No need, sir. I will just ... just...'

Simon looked up at her. 'Are you unwell?'

Her face had gone pale, and she suddenly turned to the side and began to retch. Then she vomited.

For a moment Simon was unsure what to do, other than to quickly stand and step back in case she vomited on his boots.

Henshaw came darting through the curtain and bent solicitously by his daughter.

'I ... I am sorry, sir,' Jane said between deep breaths. 'Father, I fear I must lie down.'

Henshaw quickly made apologies to Simon and gently shepherded him through the curtain into the shop where others were awaiting their turn. 'I am sorry, good folk,' said Henshaw. 'My daughter is overtired from seeing so many people. She needs to rest.'

As Simon followed the others outside, he determined that he would give her a few days and he would make enquiries around the town and gather some testimonies from people she had supposedly given healing to. Then, if actual cures did not occur, he would summons her as planned and add his own evidence of charlatanry.

He headed along Finkle Street and on towards the Northgate, one of the three main streets, to the tavern were he knew he could get a bowl of good pottage and a mug of strong ale. He chuckled to himself as he went, wondering if the sight of his pustules and blackheads had turned the girl's stomach.

He did not look behind him and so did not see the figure who was following him.

Refreshed after eating and slaking his thirst, he spent the afternoon tracking four of the eight men that had allegedly been part of the mob that had damaged the doors of St John's Priory on the day of the attack upon the Constable of Pontefract, when the two men had been killed. One was a fuller, two were millers and the fourth was a ditcher. All four looked to be strong young men, who could potentially be troublesome when they were issued with summonses, so he decided to delay serving them until he had engaged two of the former soldiers he had employed before. There was no sense in taking unnecessary risks, he felt.

While he was up at the top of the town he decided to take the opportunity to visit St John's Priory, which stood near the castle, not far from the execution ground of Thomas of Lancaster, where Jane the Healer claimed she had seen the martyred earl. Even at this time of the day the area was swarming with pilgrims, both around the great cross that had been erected where the block had been, and around the gates of the priory. All manner of votive offerings had been left at both sites.

There is certainly more interest here than when I was last in Pontefract, Simon mused. As he walked past the cross, he saw several people kneeling before it in prayer. 'Who do you pray for?' he asked a man in a smock as he rose from his knees.

'Why, for sainted Thomas, of course,' he replied.

The man next to him also rose. 'And I pray for Jane the Healer, who has been taken ill.'

Simon was surprised that news had travelled so fast.

'She cured my old mother's palsy last week,' a young man said, eager to tell his tale. 'We are fortunate to live in such a blessed place as Pontefract.'

The first man nodded in agreement. 'Aye, but it is not so blessed for them that were cursed by your St Thomas. Perkin Cratwell, he that wielded the axe that cut off Thomas's head, is dead. And by his own hand.'

The young man looked sideways and spat. 'Cratwell had much blood on his hands, so he won't be missed much. But those others that were cursed and are still alive had best pray for their souls, too.'

A crowd formed as others gathered and freely offered their opinions.

Simon knew that it was King Edward and his chamberlain, Hugh le Despenser, that references were being made to, albeit without any mention of names. He knew that such gatherings could be dangerous places for loose talk, for no one knew when a king's spy could be near and one could be denounced for treason. He remained silent and moved away, having heard enough. There was certainly ill feeling against King Edward and the King's Eye and by contrast, much love for the memory of the executed Earl of Lancaster.

The priory gatehouse had a double arch in its high walls. A large one designed for carts was closed, but the smaller one for walkers was open. Although made of stout timber, it bore signs of recent damage with swords or axes or such. Following a stream of people, he entered the enclosure and crossed the cobbled close to pass the chapter house, vestry and cloister to gain entry to the church. As with the outer gate, this too bore evidence of damage and recent repair.

Inside, there was already a crowd of people who were all eager to approach, touch and pray at the tomb of the earl, which stood at the right side of the high altar. As he looked around at the faces, he recognised the same devoted and hopeful expressions as he had seen waiting upon Jane the

Healer. He took his turn and made a show of reverence at the tomb, so that he appeared to be one of the pilgrims.

Then at the rear of the nave he spied what he hoped to see, two monks dressed in the black robes of their order, taking money and handing over tiny clay bottles to several of these pilgrims.

Ah, I have caught these fellows in the act of simony, he mused and made his way across to them.

'Good fathers, have you any relics of blessed Thomas that I may purchase to help cure my skin condition?' he asked, pointing at his face.

The older of the two, an elderly monk, bowed, showing his tonsured pate. 'My brother is from our mother priory in France and speaks only a little English, my son. And of course, for a small offering you may have one of these clay pots containing a hair from the head of the sainted Thomas.'

'*Et aussi*,' said the other, also bowing, '*le sang du saint.*'

The elderly monk smiled and patted the other's shoulder. And more to him than to Simon, he said, 'The blood of the saint.' He took the pot from the French monk and shook it, producing a slight rattle inside. 'These contain earth upon which his blood fell.'

'I will have one of each,' Simon replied, reaching inside his purse. 'May I have your names, fathers?'

'I am Brother Thaddeus and this is Brother Jean-Claude,' replied the elder.

Simon's smile dropped as soon as he had purchased the pots and deposited them inside his satchel. 'Then Brother Thaddeus and Brother Jean-Claude, know you that I am Simon of Holderness, Summoner to the York Consistory Court. I need you to take me at once to your prior, for I have summonses for you both on charges of simony and blasphemy.'

Simon was in excellent spirits the next morning, for he had sketched out a plan in his mind. He would once again seek out those that he had seen at Henshaw the girdler's shop and see if he could find out what they were doing in Pontefract. It was as yet a mystery to him, but one he was determined to solve. But first, he would spy again upon Jane Henshaw the Healer and glean more evidence of her charlatanry.

Once more he made his way to Walkergate to see if people were visiting Jane the Healer again. It was a surprise to find plenty of confused people milling around, and the girdler's shop was closed and bolted.

He asked some disappointed people why the shop was closed.

'The girl was taken ill in the night,' a man with a lazy eye told him. 'She started having fits and had a flux of the bowels, so they say.'

'The apothecary couldn't help, for she could not be made to swallow his physic.'

'Her father took her to the hospital,' said another.

'St Nicholas's Hospital?' Simon asked. He planned to follow her, for he needed to ensure that there was no question about her and her father absconding from Pontefract before he could issue a summons to each of them. Yet why would they? He had not revealed himself as a summoner to them.

'No, her father did not think he could carry her up the hill that far. He took her by cart to St Mary Magdalene's Hospital. The nuns there will see anyone who is gravely ill.'

Simon cringed, for he knew that the hospital was close to a Lazar House, where lepers lived and were treated. As a sufferer from a skin condition himself, he was only too thankful that in comparison to leprosy, his ailment was nothing. He mumbled thanks for the information and went to get Jethro to ride out of town to St Mary Magdalene's Hospital, a journey of about a mile and a half on the road towards the village of Darrington.

The road climbed uphill quite steeply and then flattened out. He passed woods and then came upon a cleared area. He recoiled at the stench of a desiccated corpse hanging from the town gibbet that he passed on his left. Jethro, sensing proximity to the dead body, attempted to stop, but the summoner prodded him on, allowing him to veer to the edge of the trail as he picked up his pace. Soon after they came to a crossroads close to St Mary Magdalene's Hospital, a moderate-sized compound with a fairly low wall surrounding it, with a tower, chapter house and the hospital buildings attached to a chapel.

He shuddered inwardly as some two hundred yards distant on the far side of the crossroads, as most leper hospitals were built, he sighted the Lazar House with a much higher wall, closed gates and the roof of a separate chapel, as was common in leper compounds. Once again, he felt relieved that he was not having to visit there.

Tethering Jethro at the gates of the hospital, he went in and knocked hard on the front door. It was opened to him by a nun. She was clearly distressed.

Revealing that he was a Church official from the York Consistory Court, rather than saying he was a summoner, he told her that he'd come to visit Jane the Healer.

'Have you not heard? Jane Henshaw died in the night. Her father had left her with us and returned home, but he was sent for when we found her after Vigils at six bells. He is with her now, and they are being looked after by one of the sisters.'

'What ... what happened?' Simon asked, shocked at the news. 'I heard that she just had a flux of the bowel?'

'That is what we thought, but she started to have fits and they became more and more violent. She was having one after the other, so she was nursed in a single cell on her own. But she did not improve and Mother Cecilia, our Mother Superior, sent one of the novices to find a friar to give her the last rites, in case she died suddenly. The poor girl seemed to have lost her sight for she was screaming that she couldn't see. Fortunately, a friar was passing by outside and he came at once. He asked us to leave her with him, and he prayed over her. After a while he came out and said that the Lord had helped her and she had fallen asleep and should be left undisturbed. Well, after Vigils I was sent to check on her and I ... I found her dead by ... by her own hand!'

She suddenly broke down and covered her face with her hands. Simon waited awkwardly as she sobbed for a few moments before recovering a little.

'It was horrible, sir. Before the friar calmed her, she had been crying out about not being able to see between these fits. She was still wearing her apron, and during a fit she must have stabbed at both her eyes with a bodkin. There was blood and eye jelly over her face and a large bodkin in her clenched hand was sticking straight through her eye. It must have gone into her brain.'

Simon of Holderness suddenly wished that he had not told them that he was a Church official of the York Consistory Court, for a self-murder was not something that he could ignore. It was a sin that would have profound implications for her family and for the hospital. Strictly speaking, as a sudden and unexpected death it should be reported immediately to the coroner, but this was a death on Church soil and not the death of an ordinary person at that. If Jane Henshaw had been given the gift of healing by one who might actually be a saint, then the opinion of his master the dean would be vital.

'Calm yourself, Sister —?'

'Veronica, sir. I am Sister Veronica.'

'And I am a summoner to Walter Lydford, Dean of St Salvator's Church and Commissary General of the York Consistory Court. I do not have his knowledge of ecclesiastical law, but I have some legal learning. I had better see the body, then we must decide what has to be done.'

It was then that he heard a man crying. Somehow he just knew that he was going to be kept busy, especially if this could be considered a case of self-murder.

Harald Barrowman had run the Pikestaff Inn for twenty years and enjoyed his ale, especially when a customer was happy to pay for him to drink with him. The one-legged man with the crutches told him that he was a pilgrim and that he had just made an offering at the Priory of St John the Evangelist, and that it had been recommended that he stay at the tavern for a couple of nights before making his way back to Coventry.

As they drank their sixth mug together, he asked about how many other people were staying and whether they too were pilgrims.

This caused Harald such amusement that he laughed until tears ran down his cheeks. 'No, friend, there is just the one other and he certainly is no pilgrim.'

Then his newfound drinking companion told him that he had once been a monk and that he had absconded from his monastery and had been excommunicated, which was why he had become a pilgrim by way of atonement. That was when Harald told him to be careful around his other guest, because he was actually a summoner and would as like as not give him a summons and drag him off to the Church Court in York.

Thanking him, the fellow had paid him for two nights and let Harald show him to his bed, which was curtained off like the other, where he had immediately gone to lie down.

The tavern became very busy as the day wore on and Harald drank more ale. He entirely forgot to say anything about the new guest when Simon of Holderness returned later that day.

CHAPTER SIX

Richard and Hubert had reached Pontefract before nightfall and made their way uphill to the rocky outcrop on which stood the honey-coloured stones of Pontefract Castle. The guards at the barbican gates informed them that Sir Clifford de Mosley, the Constable of Pontefract Castle, had ordered that they were to be admitted and afforded the hospitality of the castle.

'It is a far mightier castle than Sandal, my lord,' said Hubert, looking around the vast inner bailey once they had dismounted.

'It is larger, certainly, and there is almost a village behind these great walls. The garrison alone holds close on a hundred men, according to His Majesty, and it can comfortably house six hundred in all. It has trebuchets, couillards and ballistas for protection and just look at the battlements and those seven towers. Built as it is up on this rock, it is virtually impregnable, and assuming its wells do not dry out could withstand a siege for a year, in my opinion.'

An ostler took their horses and two servants took their saddlebags and baggage, one taking Hubert's to the barracks block and another taking Richard's to the keep, where two chambers on the second storey had been prepared for him. Another runner simultaneously set off to the magnificent building that was clearly the constable's house, and within moments he brought a page scuttling across to greet them.

The page pulled off his cap and bowed deeply. 'Greetings and welcome to Pontefract Castle, Sir Richard. I am Martin of Helmsley, page to Sir Clifford de Mosley. My master presents his compliments, but he is unable to greet you personally. He is

101

still recovering from his recent attack and is asleep abed under the orders of Doctor Jessop, his physician.'

'Are Sir Clifford's injuries bad?' Richard asked.

The page, a lad of around sixteen years, nodded. 'He was struck with a stone and knocked from his horse, Sir Richard. Doctor Jessop has been treating his broken leg and his head wound and orders that he must rest as much as possible. The doctor has bled him today. I am instructed to tell you that he must sleep tonight, but he will attend on you tomorrow morning.'

Richard clicked his tongue and frowned in slight irritation. He had wished to consult with the constable so that he could begin gathering information and start his investigations into the death of Perkin Cratwell and the alleged cult of Thomas of Lancaster straight away.

Seeing his displeasure, Martin of Helmsley smiled nervously. 'But if you please, Sir Richard, I am instructed to tell you that in my master's absence Lady Justina, Sir Clifford's wife, is hosting a meal that she would like you to attend, as tonight is the feast of the Stigmata of St Francis. Many of the dignitaries and clerics of the area will be attending.'

Richard dismissed Hubert and followed Martin to his chambers in the keep.

A formal dinner I could do without, he thought. *Yet it could prove useful to get to know the local gentry and clerics.*

The keep was an impressive three-storey edifice consisting of three conjoined drum towers in quatrefoil plan, built upon an already impressively raised motte. Each storey of the keep, explained Martin of Helmsley as he outlined the geography of the castle, contained five chambers. The ones allotted to Richard were spacious and faced towards the town of

Pontefract and its older Saxon township of Tanshelf. Torches in the walls of the spiral staircase gave the honey stone a warm glow.

After unpacking his saddlebags and arranging his writing equipment on the large oak table that he proposed to use as a desk, Richard availed himself of his private garderobe, performed his ablutions and then pulled on the garter that Wilhelmina had given him, as she had told him to wear it. With a sigh he pushed thoughts of her from his mind and lay down to think about the mission that his king had sent him on. Yet following his work in court, his meeting with the King and the long journey to Pontefract, he soon fell into a deep sleep, wherein his visions and thoughts were only of Lady Wilhelmina.

He was reluctantly roused from slumber by the peal of six bells from somewhere within the castle grounds. He dressed himself in fresh hose and breeches, a blue tunic and darker blue half-cape and pulled on a pair of calf leather boots. Using a burnished metal mirror above the large wooden chest where he had stored his belongings, he ran his fingers through his hair and combed it into place as best he could. Finally, he buckled on a belt with a stiletto and his personal food-knife, before opening the door to let himself out of the chamber.

Martin the page was waiting patiently by the door. 'I have come to escort you to the Great Hall, Sir Richard,' he said, bowing and stretching his hand towards the stairs.

A light drizzle had begun to fall as they crossed the bridge over the inner moat to the vast inner bailey and headed across it towards the chapel of St Clements, the old Saxon chapel that had been added to by the first Normans below the King's Tower. Richard looked up at the battlement walls where sentries were moving back and forth between towers, just as they would throughout both the day and night. A slight chill accompanied the rain, and he was glad that he was going to be heading indoors into the warmth to enjoy food and wine and learn something of Pontefract.

A short flight of steps led up to the main door and a corridor, at the end of which two guards stood to attention. Martin led the way and tapped at the door, which was immediately opened by a liveried servant. He bowed to Richard and turned to announce him.

'Sir Richard Lee, the Circuit Judge of His Majesty King Edward's Northern Realm.'

The Great Hall was full of people sitting on highbacked wooden chairs on either side of two rows of linen-covered trestle tables arranged along the length of the room. The servant then bowed and held out a hand for Richard to follow him along the hall to the top table, where several people were seated, facing the other guests. Torches spluttered along the walls, each emitting an oily smoke, while the rain beat against the greenish glazed glass of six large mullioned windows which faced the bailey. A fire blazed in a great hearth beneath the newly fashioned coat of arms of King Edward the Second of Caernarvon. It was apparent that the arms of the House of Lancaster had been replaced almost immediately after the earl had been executed.

Richard acknowledged the greetings and the gestures of welcome as he passed the lesser tables, occupied by the burghers and guildmasters of Pontefract and their wives. The top table was reserved for Lady Justina and the local dignitaries and clerics.

All of the men at the top table stood up as a petite lady in a wimple and green gown smiled and touched the vacant seat next to her.

Richard bowed to them all. 'Lady Justina, I thank you for inviting me to share in this meal. I am only sorry that your husband is still unwell from his recent injuries.'

A good-looking lady in her early forties, Richard guessed, she smiled demurely as he took his seat. 'It pains him, I assure you, Sir Richard, but he is under the orders of his physician, Doctor Jessop. Yet he is determined that he will attend on you in the morning.'

She clapped her hands and a servant nearby took this as the signal to start the feast. He produced a bell from a voluminous sleeve and shook it once. Immediately, a quartet of musicians in a minstrel's gallery above the top table began to play. Soon the air was filled with the music of harp, vielle, olander and lute. At a second ring of the bell, the side doors opened and a team of servants filed in, led by a butler who began directing his subordinates with almost military precision.

A pantler and two assistants began serving trenchers for all the guests, and finger bowls for every two people. Then a stream of serving women followed with salvers of cut meats, steaming pots and jugs of wine and ale.

'This feast, if that is the word to use for such simple fare as we have to offer, was my idea, Sir Richard,' Lady Justina went on. 'There seems to be a stirring of unwanted forces in the land, and today is the celebration of the Stigmata of St Francis of Assisi. Which is why I have invited our guests from the different holy orders and other distinguished guests. Allow us to introduce ourselves to you beginning from the far left.'

'I am Prior Stephen of Cherobles, the Prior of St John the Evangelist,' said a middle-aged man with a wise face, dressed in a black habit with a matching scapulary. He bowed his tonsured head and smiled. 'I will join you in eating, but I am afraid that my order prohibits all flesh food, so I shall only avail myself of a few vegetables. Likewise, I must forego the wine from the castle cellar but will instead indulge in Adam's ale.' To prevent any wine being poured into his goblet, he overturned it, so that the server would understand that he wanted only water.

Richard laughed softly. 'Well said, Prior Stephen. Water flowed in abundance in Eden, and if it was good enough for the first man and his wife, then —'

'— then it is a good thing that we live in the present,' interjected the man beside the prior, clean-shaven and in his early thirties. He chuckled and introduced himself. 'I am Sir Baldwin de Ilkley and this is my wife, Lady Elizabeth. I certainly will be enjoying the feast, since I have taken no vows of abstinence.' To demonstrate, he raised a goblet over his shoulder so that it could be filled. As soon as it was charged he took a hefty sip, then wiped his mouth with the back of his hand and smiled. 'Of any kind,' he added, winking at Richard, as he put his hand on the wrist of the stunningly blue-eyed lady sitting next to him. In her turn, she gave him an irritated look and then smiled apologetically at Richard.

'My husband has the humour of the alehouse and sometimes half the wit of the most drunken sot there.'

Sir Baldwin stared at her with an open mouth for a second and then burst into a raucous laugh. 'She is right there, Sir Richard. No fripperies about me. I'm a north countryman born and bred and proud of it, so I speak my mind.'

'A laudable thing,' replied Richard, 'as long as one thinks about the consequences of one's words first.'

Lady Justina laughed lightly and waited until the pantler had placed a trencher before her, then she held a hand towards the man sitting to her right. He was not dressed so richly as Sir Baldwin, yet he still looked prosperous. He wore a gold chain of office around his neck. Beside him a rather prim-looking woman with a retroussé nose and slight dimple in her chin was chatting to a friar who wore a black mantle over a white habit. The headborough and his wife were both in their early forties, Richard estimated. The friar, he thought, was probably about ten years or so older and was clearly a Dominican, one of the Black Friars of Pontefract.

'This is Rupert Shenley, the Headborough of Pontefract,' said Lady Justina. 'And this is Mistress Bernice Shenley, his wife.'

The lady looked round at the mention of her name and both she and her husband nodded at Richard. 'We have heard of you, Sir Richard,' Rupert Shenley said. 'If I as the headborough can be of assistance, you have only to call on me.'

'Rupert has done great work and has made several reforms which have helped the needy of the town,' Lady Justina volunteered. 'He is a great help to my husband.'

The headborough shook his head apologetically. 'Although I am afraid that I could not help him much when that mob of pilgrims attacked him and his men.'

Richard gave a shrug of his shoulders. 'A mob means an unruly gathering, Master Shenley. As I understand it, they were incensed and there were too many to be contained. From what I have heard, it is fortunate that things did not get even more out of hand.'

'True, Sir Richard. I was not actually present at the attack, but it grieves me that we lost two good men and that Sir Clifford is still suffering from his injuries.'

Lady Justina repeated her earlier statement. 'My husband will attend on you tomorrow, Sir Richard. I am sure that Master Shenley will give you whatever help you need in the town.'

'Yes, indeed. I do try and keep all of the guildmasters and their members content,' he said, pointing at the other guests on the lower two tables. 'We have good relations between all of the trades. I myself am a wool merchant and guildmaster of the wool merchants. Before I was honoured to take public office I used to travel much myself, westwards across the Pennines as far as Whalley Abbey and even to Lancaster Priory, then all the way east, using the waterways from Knottingley along the Rivers Aire and the Ouse and thence on to Hull and Beverley.'

'You must miss seeing the land,' Richard remarked. 'The wool trade is so important to the country's wealth.'

Rupert Shenley gave an emphatic nod of his head. 'I have to admit that I do, Sir Richard. I enjoyed negotiating with the landowners, the abbots and priors for their clip of wool and I enjoyed bargaining with the fullers and weavers.' He gave a short laugh. 'But I do not miss travelling over the Pennines in the pouring rain. Nowadays, I enjoy administration and my duties within Pontefract, where there is much work to be done.'

His wife, Bernice, leaned forward. 'He is even trying to persuade some of the guilds to take women on as apprentices, Sir Richard.'

'Indeed,' Richard replied. 'Then that would put Pontefract ahead of most towns. It is a matter that I think needs addressing in the statute books. As it is, if a family only has daughters, then none of them may enter a skilled occupation or trade as an apprentice, merely as an unskilled helper, no matter how skilled they become.'

'It is good to hear that you are sympathetic, Sir Richard,' said the headborough. 'We have a case in point at this moment. A young girl is a helper to her father, one of our local girdlers. She is as skilled as any apprentice, yet will not be able to carry on her trade if her father dies unless she marries one who is a member of the guild.'

'And yet,' said the friar, a man of about sixty, 'this girl has been singled out for divine help.' He bowed his head, revealing his tonsured crown. 'I am Father Friar Alfred, the Friar in Chief of St Richard's Friary, which is below the town. You will have passed us in the valley to the right of the road as you entered the town.'

'Divine help, you say, Father Alfred?' Richard asked. 'Tell me more.'

The friar clicked his tongue. 'This girl saw a vision of blessed Thomas at the place he was executed on the Monk's Hill. Since then, she has been blessed with the gift of healing.'

'Pah! There is no such thing,' said Sir Baldwin. 'There is too much talk of saints and visions and healing in Pontefract these last few months. Show me this saint and I'll heal a few of these pilgrims with a good birch, the back of my hand or my boot.'

Prior Stephen remonstrated. 'Perhaps you should follow the good advice given to you by Sir Richard before you speak, Sir Baldwin.'

'It is true, husband,' said Lady Elizabeth. 'And you have not yet supped even a single flask of wine.'

The knight opened his mouth to reply, but was silenced by Lady Justina, who clapped her hands. 'I think we can talk more, but your food is getting cold, so please, eat and enjoy our table.'

The meal passed in congenial fashion as the diners at the top table drifted into polite conversation. It was only after several courses that Richard felt able to steer it back to the subject of the girl, Jane Henshaw, and her vision.

'News of her vision of blessed Thomas of Lancaster has spread wide and far,' said Friar Alfred. 'People would come to see her if it was merely a case of seeing the sainted Thomas, but since that vision she has also been given the power to heal, so the numbers of pilgrims to Pontefract has trebled.'

'It has indeed,' agreed Prior Stephen from the other end of the table. 'The same thing has happened at the site of his martyrdom and also at my priory.'

Sir Baldwin snorted derisively, but held his counsel when Richard saw Lady Elizabeth touch his hand.

'It can only be a good thing,' said Friar Alfred. 'It means that people are turning to our Lord, even if it is through his new acolyte, Thomas of Lancaster. My friars are constantly being stopped and asked about spiritual matters by all of these pilgrims.'

Rupert Shenley sipped from his goblet and then delicately dabbed his lips with the back of his hand. 'I might suggest that this is also good for the coffers of the town of Pontefract. Our tradesmen and businesses thrive with this extra income that is being brought in.'

Sir Baldwin guffawed, much to the obvious irritation of his wife. 'Of course, we all knew that some young girl was going to have such a vision.'

'How so, Sir Baldwin?' Richard asked.

Pleased to have people listening to him again, the knight went on. 'We have a hermit in Pontefract who does nothing but sit in a cave and pray and make prophesies. Have you heard of him?'

'I have only just arrived, Sir Baldwin.'

The knight nodded curtly. 'So you have. He's famous in these parts, is Peter the Hermit. He told some of the people who bring him food that firstly Thomas of Lancaster would become a saint and that soon a girl would have a vision of him.' He snorted, trying hard to suppress a further laugh of derision.

'It is true what Sir Baldwin says,' Father Friar Alfred said. 'Peter the Hermit has carved out a hermitage from a cave in the sandstone cliff below Southgate, not far from our friary. It is more than a cave, for he apparently has several chambers within it, including his living chamber at the bottom of a spiral staircase that he has hewn and where there is a well. I remember when he came about half a dozen years ago and found the ancient cave, which he gradually created into his hermitage. He lives by charity alone and is rarely seen beyond the opening of his hermitage. Often the doors are closed, but when he has experienced messages in sleep or during prayer, he is willing to tell any who visit. He himself had a vision that foretold that a girl would have a vision just as Sir Baldwin said.'

Richard ran a finger over his moustache. 'Interesting. So tell me, what did she see?'

'She saw the blessed Thomas surrounded by light,' Friar Alfred replied. 'He told her not to be afraid but to kneel so that he could anoint her head. He did so and she immediately felt the healing power course through her blood into her very fingertips. And then she fell into a deep sleep and was discovered by one of Prior Stephen's monks.'

'So it is apt that this evening we should have the feast to the Stigmata of St Francis of Assisi,' said Lady Justina. 'St Francis also had the healing gift after his vision.'

Richard pointed to a couple of wolfhounds that were dozing in the heat of the great hearth at the end of the hall. 'I understood that St Francis could heal animals and birds.'

'That is correct,' said Friar Alfred. 'But he received his gift from Jesus Christ. After he saw the Lord, he developed the stigmata.'

'The stigmata?' Richard repeated.

'He developed the wounds of Christ, the marks of the nails on his wrists and ankles where the Lord had been nailed to the cross when he was crucified.'

'And also the wound in his side, where the Lord was stabbed with a spear,' Prior Stephen continued. 'He had the vision two years before he died and he carried these wounds with him unto his grave. All that time he was blessed with the gift of healing. It is said that his wounds never stopped bleeding, and his clothes were often blood-soaked.'

'It must have been a strange phenomenon,' Richard said. 'Can it be accounted for by physicians?'

'No,' replied Friar Alfred. 'Why should it? It is not something of this earth, but instead is caused by the divine. Just like the vision that the child Jane Henshaw had of blessed Thomas.'

Richard sat up straight, assuming a more assertive manner. 'And yet His Majesty the King had Thomas of Lancaster executed as a traitor. How is it that there is talk at this table of him being blessed and saintly and having been martyred?'

'Forgive us, Sir Richard,' said Prior Stephen, 'but perhaps we who have taken holy orders are more in tune with the divine than is our sovereign.'

Richard went on, 'And yet His Majesty is the anointed King of England. Surely that means that he is chosen by God?' He noted that Prior Stephen's lips tightened and he sat back in his chair. 'Then there is talk of a curse made by Thomas of Lancaster.'

'And of deaths from it,' Sir Baldwin volunteered.

'Do you know of deaths here in Pontefract as a result of it?'

112

'I suggest keeping our voices down,' Lady Justina said. 'Our other guests may be alarmed with talk of the curse. My husband may be the best person to talk to about this, Sir Richard.'

Richard looked over at the other tables, where all seemed to be enjoying the feast and the wine that seemed to be poured in abundance. He smiled at Lady Justina and continued in a hushed tone. 'And then there is talk of another curse.'

'The one in Carlisle?' Sir Baldwin said. 'Aye, by the Earl of Carlisle. I heard that before he died he cursed the memory of Lancaster and cursed all who had been party to bringing him low. And who can say they don't war against each other? The curses, I mean.'

'Again, Sir Richard,' said Lady Justina, 'my husband may have knowledge of this.'

'Indeed,' said Richard, reluctant to have his line of questioning diverted by the constable's wife. 'But going back to the stigmata, it interests me, this wounding without cause and this everlasting bleeding. I wonder if it is like that other unfathomable but presumably divine cause of bleeding. Cruentation!'

'What is cruentation, Sir Richard?' Lady Elizabeth asked nervously.

'It is a strange thing,' Richard replied. 'I have seen it happen several times in cases of murder. A dead body will bleed in the presence of the person who killed them.'

Lady Elizabeth shivered. 'Oh, what a horrible thing to happen.'

Sir Baldwin put a hand on his wife's shoulder and squeezed as he gave a gruff laugh. 'Lady Elizabeth is very impressionable, and such things frighten her. But surely such a thing is not possible, Sir Richard.'

'I have heard of it,' said Prior Stephen. 'I have no difficulty accepting such a thing. After all, we live in the world that God made, and this would be something that the Lord has given us to show sin.'

Bernice Shenley leaned forward. 'And where would the body bleed from, Sir Richard? From a wound?'

'If the death was a result of violence, then that is likely. In the case of poison, it may cause bleeding from other body orifices.'

'It sounds more like something Satan would cause to happen, rather than God,' said Lady Justina.

Sir Baldwin laughed again. 'It is just as well that the *murderer* doesn't bleed. That way, Perkin Cratwell would have been bled every day of his life.'

'Perkin Cratwell?' Richard repeated innocently, though he was grateful to hear the name mentioned without saying it himself.

'He was the executioner,' said Sir Baldwin. 'He was both the public and the royal executioner until one of those curses got him. He hanged himself. Good riddance, I say!'

'Why say you that?' Richard asked.

'The man was a disgrace to Pontefract. He revelled in his work and sent many good people to their deaths,' Sir Baldwin grimaced as if he suddenly had a bad taste in his mouth. He took a hefty swig of wine and put his goblet down heavily.

'We should not speak ill of the dead, Sir Baldwin,' said Father Friar Alfred. 'Remember that he committed a sin by taking his own life and has been excommunicated. He lies in non-consecrated soil as a result.'

Lady Elizabeth shivered again. 'Does ... does that mean he could rise again and m-murder people?'

Sir Baldwin patted her hand. 'No, his spirit will be roasting in Hell and the worms will be feasting on his flesh at this very minute.'

'He will not be missed in Pontefract, Sir Richard,' Rupert Shenley the headborough volunteered. 'He had been given *droit de havage* by His Majesty, and he used it at every opportunity. Why, he scarcely ever paid for anything, causing much loss to the businesses and shopkeepers of Pontefract. Ask any of the townspeople and you will find few willing to mourn him.'

Richard picked up his goblet and sipped thoughtfully. *It appears that the only person who held the executioner in high regard was King Edward himself.*

'We took a great risk meeting here at this hour,' said the woman as the four sat around a table. 'We should only meet at the other place.'

The older man waved his hand in dismissal. 'Do you think I am comfortable coming here? All that we do is a risk, but it must be done.'

'I agree,' said the youngest man. 'I take the most risks, but without me all is a waste of time.'

'Take care what you say,' warned the woman. 'We take risks every time we venture outside.' She looked to the third man for support.

He nodded and eyed the younger. 'Don't you forget that if it was not for us, this would never have been possible.'

'Stop squabbling!' snapped the oldest. 'Has the latest danger been removed?'

'Of course,' came the reply. 'With your help, two birds have now been killed with the same stone, and the stone itself has been removed.'

'Good. And what about this new threat that has suddenly come to us?'

'It will be dealt with if necessary.'

'Without blood?'

A cruel laugh escaped cold lips. 'That I cannot guarantee. Sometimes letting blood is a necessary pleasure.'

CHAPTER SEVEN

'Miracles, Sir Richard!' exclaimed Sir Clifford de Mosley, the Constable of Pontefract Castle, as the two men sat opposite each other in de Mosley's office in the Blanche Tower the morning after the feast of the Stigmata of St Francis. The constable was sitting with a heavily bound lower leg supported on a stool. 'A plague on the stupid simpletons who believe in them and upon those who spread the news of each fresh one.'

'Have there been many such reports?'

The constable reached for his goblet of wine. 'Too many! They began within days of Thomas of Lancaster's execution. The first was a blind priest who said that on three successive nights the earl came to him in a dream and told him to visit the hill that was the place of execution. He did so and rubbed soil from the spot on his eyes and then claimed that his sight had been restored.'

'And had it?'

The constable took a deep draught of wine and rubbed the jagged, healing scar over his right eye, the remnant of the wound he had received from a stone when he had been attacked some weeks before. He was a stocky, gruff-looking man with a straggly moustache and beard and the scar caused him to half close his eye, giving him a perpetually cynical look. 'He could see, but the question is, had he ever been blind? He was not a priest of the town but a wandering friar, so I have no way of knowing.' He clicked his tongue. 'We have too many of these mendicant friars in this town already without the droves of them that have come lately.'

'That was just the first miracle, though?' Richard queried.

'If you must use that word,' the constable replied, plaintively. Then he told him of several other reports, including a child who had drowned in a well near the marketplace. 'After three days and nights of praying and hoping, his kinfolk took his body to the priory and laid it on the tomb of Thomas of Lancaster, whereupon the child revived. The child must have been in a deep sleep, but of course, they all said it was a miracle.' He drank more wine. 'And of course,' he went on, 'there have been cases of folk said to be afflicted with madness being cured, and of lame beggars having their paralysed limbs restored.'

Sir Richard glanced at the King's warrant that he had presented to Sir Clifford. It lay where the constable had tossed it down in a fit of displeasure at being effectively relieved of his post as the authority in Pontefract. Richard had expected such a reaction, especially since His Majesty had also told him that he and his man, Hubert of Loxley, should be furnished with accommodation and given access to however many men he considered necessary for his investigations.

Instead of starting proceedings immediately, Richard and Hubert had decided to familiarise themselves with the castle, the town and its many religious houses. First, Richard had started by going over the reports of all the miraculous events that the constable knew about.

'You are not a believer in these miracles, Sir Clifford?' he asked.

'I am not. I am sure that the so-called *cured* beggars will again become infirm so that they can beg anew before experiencing yet another miraculous cure, the mad will sink back into their madness and the deaf who started to hear will again become deaf. I believe in the physic that Doctor Jessop gives me, although I dislike it when he opens a vessel in my arm and bleeds me.' He rubbed absentmindedly at his forearm, which was also bound heavily, evidence of the physician's recent treatment. As he did, Richard noted how pale the constable looked, presumably from the bloodletting.

'How do you account for the fact that so many claim to have been made well?'

Sir Clifford shrugged. 'I don't know, but I do not like it. I believe in our Lord Jesus Christ and in all that the Bible tells us, but the Earl of Lancaster was executed as a traitor. I knew of him before his death, and he was far from being a saint.' His eyebrows beetled. 'And ever since then we have been plagued by pilgrims, literally hundreds of them. They come every day to visit the site of his execution, what they call his place of martyrdom, and then they visit his tomb, which they call a shrine. The monks erected a big cross on the execution ground and it attracts pilgrims like moths to a flame.' He shook his head in disapproval.

Richard sipped his own wine. 'His Majesty told me that he commanded you to have the doors of the Priory of St John closed to stop the tomb being used as a place of worship. In attempting to carry out this order, he said that you were wounded and two of your men were killed. Sir Henry le Scrope, the Chief Justice at the time, investigated and was unable to find any of the miscreants and so no arrests were made.'

The constable shrugged. 'It was a mob. Richard Godeley and Robert de la Hawe, two good soldiers, were dragged to the ground and beaten to death. A stone hit me on the head and, stunned, I was dragged off my horse, too.' He pointed to his heavily bound leg. 'Doctor Jessop said I had a broken leg. Anyway, I was in too much pain and I could not identify individuals myself.'

Richard nodded sympathetically. 'And I understand that even now the priory has its gates open for anyone to visit the tomb, in spite of the King's wishes that it be closed. He also told me that he had ordered His Grace, William Melton the Archbishop of York, to forbid the veneration of Thomas of Lancaster at his tomb.'

Sir Clifford harrumphed. 'That is all true, but the situation here is difficult. I talked with Prior Stephen, who doesn't acknowledge the authority of Archbishop Melton, but says that as Cluniacs they owe their allegiance only to their parent abbey *La Charité-sur-Loire* in France. Also, because the gates and the priory doors had been damaged by the mob, we considered it prudent to permit pilgrims entry or risk an uprising. And we know how quickly these things can spread. It is up to the prior to discuss the matter with the archbishop. His Majesty is aware that I had to spend a week in bed recovering from my injury, which even now causes me pain and for which I have to take physic from Doctor Jessop. It sends me to sleep, which is why I could not greet you when you arrived yesterday, as you know.'

Richard smiled. 'Lady Justina hosted the meal and made me welcome. His Majesty wishes me to investigate some of these miracles and this cult that seems to be arising. When I and my man were walking through the town yesterday on our way here, we heard people openly talking about St Thomas. And there was also talk of a young girl who had seen him in a vision and had been given a healing gift as a result. Prior Stephen and Father Friar Alfred told me something of all this.'

The constable gave a grunt of derision and held up the ewer of wine, pointing it at Sir Richard's goblet.

Richard placed his hand over his goblet and shook his head. He went on, 'His Majesty is equally concerned about the curse that Thomas of Lancaster made before he died. As you know, he cursed the King and his chamberlain, Hugh le Despenser, Sir Andrew Harclay, the Earl of Carlisle and everyone that had a part in his capture, trial and execution. His Majesty told me that there had been several deaths in Pontefract and Coventry since then, including, of course, Sir Andrew Harclay's execution in Carlisle almost a year to the day after Thomas of Lancaster's. As reported to me, Lancaster had said that Andrew Harclay would die within a year. And then there is the curse that Sir Andrew Harclay made on the scaffold.' He waited a moment, carefully watching the constable's expression, which remained one of irritation and doubt. Then he added, 'His Majesty believes that sorcery could be involved in some of these deaths.'

This evoked a short laugh of disdain. 'Sorcery? Preposterous!'

'A plot to kill the King, Hugh le Despenser, and the Prior of Coventry by using the services of a necromancer known as John of Nottingham has recently been uncovered by the King's agents, and a case is being brought before the King's Bench in London. His Majesty thinks that the deaths in Carlisle and Coventry could be linked to the curse and possibly also to sorcery. He is most anxious to suppress this cult of St Thomas and to stop the rumours about this curse. If there is sorcery, then those involved must be found and dealt with like a canker on a tree.'

The constable chewed his moustache. 'What deaths have there been in Carlisle other than of Harclay the traitor?'

Richard bristled at the assumption that Sir Andrew had been a traitor, but he was determined not to show it. 'One of the headsman's assistants was found dead in an alleyway. A friar who gave Sir Andrew the last rites was found drowned in the

River Eden. A messenger who had carried the executed Earl of Carlisle's head to London never returned, but was found in a ditch having fallen from his horse and broken his neck. Similarly, another messenger who had carried the Earl's torso to Newcastle went missing and was also found with a broken neck in a forest. There was no sign of the horse.'

The constable shrugged his shoulders. 'And in Pontefract? I can't say that there have been any suspicious deaths here.'

'The King thinks otherwise. Indeed, it is mainly for this reason that he wishes me to investigate the death of Perkin Cratwell, the royal executioner.'

Sir Clifford shrugged again. 'As for that, it was self-murder. Sir Nigel Fairfax the coroner called it *felo de se*, so it is as simple as that. The man was a brute and no one in the town liked him. I imagine he became melancholic, drank himself into a fit of blackness and decided to hang himself these two weeks past.'

'Where is the body now?'

Sir Clifford frowned. 'Buried, of course. In an unmarked grave outside the town, close to the gibbet that he had hanged so many criminals from.'

He shows no sympathy for the executioner or for any of those executed, Richard thought. *Clearly, Sir Clifford sees matters as either black or white, guilty or not guilty.* 'Yet I understood that he lived in this castle?'

'Yes. His Majesty imposed favours on him and gave him free lodgings in the castle by the stables. Not only that but he had free food, ale from the kitchens and *droit de havage* throughout the town.'

'Did he claim his right?' Richard asked, although he knew well that Cratwell did from the discussion at the meal the previous night.

'All the time, which is why he wasn't popular. That and the fact that everyone knew what he did for a living, despite the hood he always wore when he was doing his work.'

'And where did he commit self-murder?'

'He took himself off to the Stump Cross on the road to Ferrybridge. A group of actors found him dangling from an arm of the cross in the morning and cut him down. They brought his body to Pontefract and were directed to the coroner's house.'

'Since His Majesty is so concerned about his death, I had better examine his lodgings and his belongings straight away.'

'As far as I know, we haven't thrown any of his belongings out yet, but we should, what with him being excommunicated now.' Sir Clifford leaned forward to pick up a bell to summon a servant.

Suddenly, there was the sound of footsteps from the stone corridor and then an urgent knocking at the door.

'Come in!' the constable barked.

The door opened and a clerk with a twisted spine that took many inches off his height shuffled in a few steps ahead of Hubert. The clerk bowed and licked his lips nervously, as if unsure whom to address. 'Sirs, I am Basil of Darrington, clerk to Sir Nigel Fairfax the county coroner.'

'I know who you are, man. What need has Sir Nigel of us?'

'He is gravely ill, sir, which is why I am here. He is paralysed, sir. I ... I am afraid that —'

'Has he been seen by a physician?' Sir Clifford snapped.

'He has been visited by Doctor Jessop, sir. He has been bled, given physic, but still I fear for him.' He raised his hand to wipe beads of perspiration from his forehead. 'The trouble is, sir, that there have been two deaths that need his urgent attention. The first is the death of Jane Henshaw the Healer.'

Hubert, standing next to the clerk, scowled at him. 'This death happened yesterday, my lords. I was in the guardhouse when the coroner's clerk here arrived just now with the news. I thought you might have need of me.'

Sir Clifford ignored Hubert, but glared at Basil of Darrington, who seemed to wither further under his gaze. 'Yesterday!' he repeated gruffly. 'How long has Sir Nigel been ill?'

The clerk clasped his hands in front of him and visibly trembled. 'Two days, sir. The girl's death was not reported until after six bells yesterday evening, sir. The girl had been taken ill the night before and removed to St Mary Magdalene's Hospital, where the nuns looked after her. She died in the early hours, and the nuns were debating —'

'Debating what?' the constable thundered impatiently, hammering his fist on his table. 'A sudden death should have been reported to the coroner without delay.'

The coroner's clerk looked distinctly uncomfortable in the face of the constable's ire. He replied tremulously, 'There was debate about whether she had killed herself. Whether she meant to stab herself or whether it was an accident.'

'She stabbed herself?' Richard queried quickly. 'A fatal wound by stabbing does not sound accidental. Tell us more.'

The clerk looked queasy. 'She had stabbed herself in both eyes, sir. That was how they found her. So they were debating with her grief-stricken father and a summoner about what to do.'

Richard nodded and held up his hand to prevent a tirade from the constable. 'I see. They did not know what to do about a death by self-murder on consecrated soil. Her father presumably wanted her to be treated with Christian reverence, and would have disputed that she had killed herself by her own hand. On the other hand, if it was self-murder, which is considered a moral abomination, the nuns would say that their house had been desecrated. Accordingly, she would have to be posthumously excommunicated. And a summoner was present, you say?'

'Yes, sir. I don't know the reason he was there, but he said that because the question of excommunication had to be considered, it would be for his master the General Commissariat of the York Consistory Court to decide.'

Richard stroked his chin. 'Indeed, it is one of the grey areas between English law and ecclesiastical law. Where is the body now?'

'She was still at the hospital last night when it was reported, sir. The summoner said the body should be removed from the building and placed outside in the garden until it could be decided whether it was self-murder or an accident, but her father would not let anyone move her. He is still with her.'

'Why was it not reported to Sir Nigel sooner?' Richard asked.

'As I understand it, sir, the summoner had said that they should wait until this morning to report the death. In the meantime, he was going to send a messenger to York. The nun who reported the death this morning said that the summoner planned to be present when the coroner saw the body today, so he could explain that he had sent to the Consistory Court for advice.'

Richard nodded, realising that the summoner had been buying time, hoping that a messenger could reach York in a day's ride, and then receive a reply after another day. 'And what of the summoner? Is he at the hospital now?'

'That's the thing, sir,' the clerk replied. 'His is the other death. His body was discovered this morning at the Pikestaff Inn by the landlord, Harald Barrowman. He had heard about

Jane the Healer's sudden death and thought the summoner should know, in case it was caused by some malignant curse. But when he went to tell him, he found him stone cold dead in his bed.'

Richard and the constable looked at each other in astonishment. After a moment, Richard asked, 'Does Sir Nigel know of all this?'

Basil of Darrington bobbed his head. 'He had heard that you were in Pontefract, sir, and he charged me to come and ask if you would intercede for him.' He shook his head. 'Sir Nigel is extremely ill, and I am worried about him, Sir Richard.'

Richard was on his feet straight away. 'I will of course intercede. This cannot wait any longer. I am sorry to hear about your master, Sir Nigel, and I hope that his physician will heal him. You can tell him that I shall call upon him in due course. But now I will see both bodies on his behalf, so tell me precisely where they are and how I get to them.'

Basil of Darrington gave him the directions and then with some relief took his leave.

Richard turned to the constable. 'I will begin with the girl's body at the hospital. Meanwhile, Sir Clifford, could you have a man go and tell the landlord of the Pikestaff Inn that I don't want anyone to touch the summoner's body until I arrive?'

The constable pointed to his bound leg. 'I would have gone myself had I been able. Of course I will.' He held up the warrant pointedly. 'I will leave these investigations to you, Sir Richard, since His Majesty has given you, his Circuit Judge, the authority to pursue these matters.' Tossing the warrant down again, he picked up the bell and rang it vigorously to summon a servant.

Richard could tell that the constable's pride had been grievously hurt, probably because the King had informed him that he was to give Sir Richard whatever assistance he needed. It seemed clear that he was not going to offer aid unless he was asked.

The sound of a man wailing was the first thing that greeted Richard and Hubert's ears when they were admitted to St Mary Magdalene's Hospital by a nun, who introduced herself as Sister Veronica, one of the eight of her order who looked after the hospital and its fifty patients and inmates.

'That is Master Henshaw you can hear,' she told them. 'He has hardly been quiet from the first moment he saw his daughter. He refuses to leave the body despite the entreaties of the summoner who visited yesterday and of Mother Cecilia, our Mother Superior.'

'Is Mother Cecilia within?' Richard asked.

'She left less than an hour ago to go to St John's Priory to discuss this situation with Prior Stephen of Cherobles. Mother Cecilia said that he is most knowledgeable about Church law and matters such as this that could lead to excommunication. The summoner said that he needed to report the situation to his master, the Dean Walter Lydford, Commissary General of the York Consistory Court, and that he would call again this morning after he had done some study of his own. He said he would send a messenger to York yesterday and that we should report the death this morning. He also said that he would return so that he would be here if the coroner should come to look at the body.' She raised her hands and slapped them against her sides in frustration. 'But he has not done so. That is why our Mother Superior has gone to seek the counsel of the prior.'

Hubert opened his mouth to make a remark, but Richard silenced him with the slightest shake of his head.

'Has the girl's body been moved?'

Sister Veronica shook her head. 'Her father will not allow anyone to touch her. The only thing he allowed was for us to cover her poor face.'

'Is anyone else with her now?'

'Sister Esmeralda is sitting with them. She is our spicer and simples compounder. And there is none more able at bleeding a vein or removing a wen as she.'

Under Richard's further questioning, Sister Veronica recounted the whole tale of Jane the Healer's admission to the hospital, her vomiting, flux of the bowels and continuous fitting, and her cries about not being able to see. Then she told him about the visit by the friar and the subsequent discovery of her body the following morning. When he was satisfied that he had all the facts, Richard indicated for the nun to lead him along the stone corridor to the cell from whence the wailing was coming from. Richard and Hubert entered and they both nodded to the nun who was sitting on a stool, fingering her rosary.

Hubert went over to the man who was kneeling by the simple pallet bed upon which the body lay, covered by a blanket to the neck and with a black sheet over the face. He placed a hand on Henshaw's shoulder and as the girdler turned, his eyes red and his cheeks tearstained, he put a finger to his lips. 'Sir Richard Lee, the Circuit Judge of the King's Northern Realm is here.'

Henshaw stopped crying and quickly stood up upon seeing Richard. 'I … I beg your leave, sir. My daughter was killed by accident. She did not kill herself willingly. I … I am sure of this.'

'I understand that you will not permit her to be moved; is that the case?' Richard asked, as sympathetically as he could.

'She must be given a Christian burial, sir. Not … not put in some hole and barred from entering Heaven. The summoner who came yesterday wanted her body moved outside.'

Sister Veronica interjected. 'Mother Cecilia suggested placing her under a bower until the decision could be made.'

'And that decision was to be made by the Consistory Court at York, is that correct?' Richard asked.

The nun nodded.

'And what exactly did the summoner say?'

'That he would arrange things today, after he made further study of the matter. He plans to return to see Mother Cecilia this morning. He must still be studying, I think.'

Hubert again looked at Richard, and was again silenced by a shake of the head.

'Master Henshaw, I need to view your daughter's body, and for that I need you to leave this cell. Sister Veronica will take you somewhere quiet.'

The girdler reluctantly allowed himself to be led out of the cell. Once the door was closed behind them, Richard pointed to the body.

'Now, Hubert, we shall see how this poor girl met her end.' So saying, he bent over the body and lifted aside the black sheet.

Despite having seen violent death on the battlefield as well as the victims of murder in many different situations, Hubert winced at the sight of the dead girl. The girl's right hand was still holding the handle of the bodkin, which was embedded in her left eye socket, right up to the handle so that none of the needle was visible. Dried blood and yellow eye jelly covered the face. The other eye had been similarly perforated, not once but several times, it seemed.

'Died by her own hand; what a thing to happen,' said Hubert.

'Hardly likely, Hubert,' Richard said. 'Even if she did this during a fit, I am doubtful that she could have done so repeatedly. And look how exactly those needle stabbings are just in her eye sockets, not on her forehead or on her nose. No, it is too precise.'

A cough from the corner of the cell reminded them that Sister Esmeralda was still with them.

'I beg your pardon, Sister,' Richard began. 'You need not be exposed to further horrors —'

With marked vigour, the nun stood and crossed to the bed. 'My pardon, Sir Richard Lee, but this was also my opinion. I wanted to tell Mother Cecilia, but this poor man's grief and anguish over his beautiful daughter's death precluded any discussion on the matter. Mother Cecilia said that I must stay and silently pray over them, so my duty has been to stay here and be quiet. But the longer I have sat and prayed, the clearer it has become that things are not as they seem.'

Richard looked down at the nun, a woman in her early forties with penetrating blue eyes that suggested shrewdness. 'You are the hospital's spicer and simples compounder, are you not, Sister Esmeralda?'

'I am, Sir Richard,' she replied with the slightest of bows.

'Do you look after the physic garden outside?'

'I do, Sir Richard. I also tend our liquorice field. I grow over thirty types of herbs and make decoctions, elixirs, unguents and all manner of potions for the patients in the hospital here. I also make salves, plaisters and medicines for the poor folk who live in the Lazar House. It is one of my duties to deliver their medicines twice a week to Father Percival, the Prior of the Lazar House, who himself has been afflicted by the disease for these past ten years.'

'So you therefore have great experience and knowledge of simples and their usage?'

Sister Esmeralda averted her eyes modestly. 'I have a copy of the *De viribus herbarum* and also *Lilium Medicinae* by the great Doctor Bernard de Gordon and use all of his recommendations. Rose burdock, wormwood, sorrel, docks, plantains, celandines — I have stocks of them all and many more in the dispensary.'

'And do you perhaps also have a knowledge of poisons?'

She raised her eyebrows and her eyes widened, as if anxious about admitting such a thing. Then she nodded. 'We use many things that are poisonous in large doses, yet which in tiny amounts are powerful curatives.'

Richard gave a wry smile. 'That is my understanding of medicine, Sister Esmeralda.' He pointed to the girl's cheeks, which even in death were bright red and mottled. Then, very carefully, he lowered the top of the girl's blouse to reveal a similar fixed flush over her throat and upper chest.

'Did you think it strange that this girl should out of nowhere start to fit the way that she did? That, together with her vomiting and flux of the bowels?'

'I did, Sir Richard. It suggested two things to me.'

This woman impresses me, Richard thought. *She is clever. Extremely clever.* 'Two poisons, perhaps?' he asked.

Hubert suddenly whistled. 'Poisons?' he asked in disbelief.

Sister Esmeralda looked down at the body of Jane the Healer and made the sign of the cross over her. 'There is a metal that is extremely poisonous but in tiny doses is a powerful remedy, and a berry that can kill if a handful are eaten, yet is also a wonderful medicine in small amounts. I believe that this girl received a compound made of both in mortal doses.'

'The berry you refer to is nightshade, is it not? It causes the redness, the rash on the skin, fever, the fits and even the troubles with vision. I have come across it before.'

Sister Esmeralda nodded grimly. 'And the other causes the flux and the vomiting.'

'Do you think it possible that in a fit she could have stabbed herself like this?' Richard asked.

Sister Esmeralda bit her lip. 'I have been wrestling with this question these past few hours, Sir Richard. I fear that great evil has been done to this poor child.'

'Do you mean evil from some curse?' Hubert asked in astonishment.

Richard and the nun simultaneously shook their heads. 'No, Hubert,' Richard replied. 'Another hand was involved here.'

'So this was murder, my lord? Pure and simple murder?' Hubert asked in disbelief.

'Someone compounded a poisonous simple,' said Sister Esmeralda. 'It is a mortal sin to make a poison in the way that one should make a medicine.'

Richard replaced the black sheet over the dead girl's face and turned to face Hubert and the nun. 'But it was a complex murder, because it was not her own hand that stabbed her eyes out and skewered her brain thus so. That was done by this mysterious friar. We need to find him and the person who made that poison and gave it to her earlier to make her convulse as violently as she did. I think it likely that more than one person was involved.'

Sister Esmeralda fingered her rosary. 'So does this mean that the poor child can receive a Christian burial, Sir Richard?'

Richard nodded. 'Yes, but not yet. Sister Esmeralda, there is some devilish plot afoot, and it is vital that it is not revealed that I know this yet. I am going to arrange for Jane Henshaw's body to be transferred to Pontefract Castle while I carry on my investigations, but I cannot say more to her father for now. We will say that we are going to await an answer from the Consistory Court in York.'

'Shall I return to the castle and have a coffin and a wagon brought here, my lord?' Hubert asked.

'Yes, Hubert, but say nothing about murder to anyone. Say that we require two men on the wagon. We need to place the body in a dungeon cell where it will be kept cool and locked securely, while we await a decision from York about whether this is self-murder or not. I will speak with Sir Clifford when I return and get him to send a messenger to York, in case the summoner did not send one himself.'

'I will attend to it at once, my lord.'

Richard scratched his chin. 'But mark this, for it is important. Have the body placed in the coffin exactly as it is without disturbing the hands or the bodkin. Cover the coffin so that once you have collected it none may disturb it. And then, after you have had the coffin taken to the dungeon in the castle, bring the wagon to the Pikestaff Inn on Skinner's Lane. If the summoner who visited her is also dead, his body will need to be removed. I will either be there or I may have gone to visit Sir Nigel Fairfax the coroner, who is apparently gravely ill.'

Once Hubert had taken his leave, Richard looked down at the diminutive nun. Considering himself a good judge of character, he had already decided to place a great trust in this shrewd woman.

'Great evil has been done here, Sister Esmeralda, as you know. But yet I fear there is even more. The summoner who came yesterday has also been found dead. I must go now and examine his body on behalf of the coroner, Sir Nigel Fairfax.'

Sister Esmeralda squeezed her rosary and made the sign of the cross. 'And he seemed in such good health yesterday. I will have to report to Sister Veronica, who is in charge in our Mother Superior's absence. Will you tell her of this awful sin that has been done under our roof?'

'I will, Sister Esmeralda, but I ask you to say nothing of it.'

The nun looked surprised. 'But both Sister Veronica and Mother Cecilia will want to know what you said. Of our conclusions about poison.'

'I am going to talk to Sister Veronica and tell her that we are removing the body to the castle while we await and discuss with the Consistory Court agents what to do. Nothing is to be gained by alarming anyone with talk of poisons at this stage. I shall phrase it so that there is no necessity for Sister Veronica or Mother Cecilia to question you. Indeed, I shall say that I think the strain has been severe upon you and that you must be allowed to rest.'

'And what of Jane's father, Master Henshaw?'

'I shall talk to him now and reassure him that his daughter will be treated with due reverence, and that we shall look after her body at the castle until I have held an inquest into her death and also discussed this with the Church authorities.'

Harald Barrowman was in a rare state of agitation as he showed Richard into the curtained booth where the body of Simon of Holderness lay just as he had found him that morning.

'Look at his face. I have never seen a look of such agony,' he said, pointing at the contorted visage, the open mouth with protruding tongue and the staring, unseeing eyes. 'I fancy it was his heart that stopped or he had an attack of apoplexy. Simon of Holderness liked to indulge in his ale and other vices. He had many of those, sir.'

'Indeed? Well, I shall come and talk to you about that, Master Barrowman,' said Richard, 'once I have had a chance to inspect his body.'

Once alone, Richard knelt in front of the summoner's corpse. He felt in the man's clothing, for he was fully dressed under the blanket apart from his discarded boots. He opened his purse and counted out a considerable sum on the floor. Under the bed, the summoner's satchel yielded several apples and carrots, a pot of ink, two quills, a penknife for their sharpening, a stack of writs, several still with the unbroken seal of Walter Lydford, Commissary General of the York Consistory Court, and others without names. There were also some palimpsests, previously used parchments that had the ink scraped off, with new names and notes in far less refined handwriting, presumably made by the summoner himself. Reaching under his pillow, Richard found a short cudgel, and in one of the boots by the bed he discovered a bollock dagger.

Richard then turned his attention to the body itself. *It looks as if he died as he was about to scream*, he mused, looking closely at the coarse features with the pustules and carbuncles, partially concealed by some form of white paste or unguent. In contrast to the white paste, the eyeballs were bloodshot and there were many broken veins about his face and around the eyes.

Richard leaned over and sniffed. *This summoner had a fondness for garlic and onions and ale*, he concluded.

He felt under the lank straggly hair and examined the back of the head. *Now this feels like a bump*, he thought as he started to turn the stiff body over to get a better view. *Indeed, it is a bruise,* and a fresh one, which means it occurred sometime before he died. It looks as if he was struck from behind and either stunned or knocked out.

He pulled the summoner's clothes up and looked at the torso, and then pulling up the sleeves, he scrutinised the arms. And here are marks on the wrists, clearly rope marks. It looks as if he had been secured. He either had his hands tied behind his back or bound in front of him.

He leaned close to the face again and nodded to himself. I think there has been a rope or a rag tied round his face, too. I can just see where this paste has been streaked.

What was it the landlord had said? He had never seen a look of such agony. Richard agreed. The face was indeed frozen in death in an expression of agony, with the swollen tongue protruding from the mouth to give the corpse a look reminiscent of a gargoyle. But there is more than that; he looks as if he is shocked and choking at the same time.

He looked closely at the throat, but saw no bruises. Perhaps nothing shows outside, but what of inside? he thought to himself. He prised open the stiff lower jaw and peered inside the mouth.

'I can't see anything,' he said to himself. 'Yet his breath smells stranger than I thought when I just smelled him earlier. It is like a mixture of garlic, onions and parchment. But why parchment?'

Looking down at the contents of the satchel, he picked up one of the quills and bent the tip around a finger until he had fashioned a sort of hook. Then he carefully inserted it into the mouth and pushed it over the tongue to the back of the palate.

'Methinks I will need to straighten your throat, friend summoner,' he mused, using both hands to push the head backwards. He began to advance the feather quill, probing as he went until he hit resistance. Then, moving the quill sideways and rotating it, he felt the quill hook dislodge something.

Slowly but surely, something was dragged up with the quill as he pulled it back. 'My God, what have we here?'

Gradually, the quill came up to reveal a yellowed bundle. Reaching into the dead man's mouth with his finger and thumb, he pulled a piece of parchment free.

'So that confirms it,' he whispered to himself. 'He was struck down, tied up to restrain him and then this was shoved down his throat. It either roused him or it was done after he had come round. He would have suffocated and died in agony and utter fear.' He further reconstructed the summoner's death in his mind. 'Then he was unbound and arranged to be found as if he had died in his bed. His murderer assumed that no one would ever discover this. So let me see what it is.'

Wiping the saliva and secretions from the bundle on the blanket, he unfurled a crumpled blank writ. 'So, it is a writ to summons someone to the Consistory Court in York. The irony is that there is no name on it. This was the summoner's death warrant, meant to silence him forever. But who was the executioner?'

CHAPTER EIGHT

After gathering the summoner's belongings, including the parchment that he had extracted from his throat, and stowing them in the satchel, Richard went downstairs and called for Harald Barrowman. The landlord nodded gratefully when Sir Richard told him that he was going to arrange for the summoner's body to be taken by wagon to Pontefract Castle and that he would deal with all of the communication with the Church Court and see that the death was duly and appropriately recorded.

'Did you have any other guests staying at your inn?'

Harald covered his mouth as if suddenly recalling something. 'Why, fool that I am, I did. A one-legged pilgrim, who had been to see the tomb of St Thomas. He paid me for his bed, in the cubicle at the other end of the room. But he wasn't there this morning when I found the summoner. I had forgotten about him, what with the shock of finding poor Simon.'

'Describe this pilgrim.'

'Not a lot to say, Sir Richard. He had one leg only, used two crutches. He was wearing a loose habit, like a lot of those pilgrims, and he had the hood up. I imagined it was because he had some disease, although I'm sure he wasn't a leper. He drank a lot of ale, sir.'

So, thought Richard. *We need to find this one-legged fellow, for undoubtedly he is the killer. But as yet I must not let this landlord know that I am aware the summoner was murdered in his inn.* 'Now tell me,' he said almost casually, 'you said that this summoner, Simon of Holderness, had many vices. What did you mean?'

'Well, Sir Richard, he liked to eat and had a partiality for onions and garlic. I don't think it did much for his skin, for it was always red and peeling, and he had crops of boils on his face. He also liked to drink ale and mead, far more than was good for him, I reckon.'

'Did he get drunk?'

'Oh yes, sir. And when he did, he would pretend to be a pious man and would babble away in Latin, showing off his learning. And he liked to talk about his work and how he made a lot of money.'

'What did he mean?'

The landlord rubbed his face with his gnarled hand and sucked air through his teeth. 'Well, sir, now that he's dead, I suppose it is only right to tell you. He was not an honest man. He threatened folk with writs, said he had the power to summons them to the Church Court for all manner of crimes against the Church. Adultery was one of the things he said it was easy to get people to pay him not to summons them for. He used to try to get me to tell him things about folk in the town.'

'And did you?'

'No, sir, not me. I don't have any cause to betray any of my neighbours or customers. But I know of some who did.'

This fellow is lying through his teeth, thought Richard. *If I give him enough rope, he may hang himself.* 'Tell me who and where I will find them.'

The landlord cast his eyes downwards, realising he had made a mistake. 'Why, sir, I don't rightly know. I ... I forget.'

'Then you had better remember quickly,' Richard replied firmly. 'If this summoner was coercing and threatening people, he was abusing his position. By withholding information, you make yourself an accessory and thereby are guilty of assisting him in extortion. Now out with it; I need names and the crimes he said they were guilty of.' Richard sat down at the table and from the summoner's satchel took out one of the palimpsests, the pot of ink and one of the quills. He slowly prepared them, aware that the landlord was manifestly rattled. 'Tell me one by one,' he ordered.

Harald Barrowman swallowed hard and then reeled off a string of names, addresses and supposed misdemeanours. Richard recorded each one carefully. 'Will ... will you tell them that I gave their names, Sir Richard?' Harald asked, anxiously.

I imagine none of these people are friends of his, mused Richard. *It will be interesting to find out if he has been truthful about them, or whether he has adopted the summoner's trickery to settle a score or two. If he has, he will pay for his sins.* 'I make no promises. Now come, do not hold back any further,' Richard replied acerbically. 'Tell me more.'

'I ... I should have said that Simon of Holderness was himself the greatest hypocrite of all, sir.'

'Explain yourself, man.'

'He ... he was a fornicator, Sir Richard. He frequently visited bawdy houses in the town and one in particular. He told me he had an arrangement with Bardolph, who runs the brothel. The summoner gave Bardolph and the bawds freedom from summonsing, and they gave him information about others who visited the house and they also serviced him for nothing. He used to brag to me that he still paid them something if he was satisfied with the pleasuring he received, as if he was being generous.'

'And these bawds, how many did he use?'

'All eight of them, at some time, sir. But he had a special favourite. Gertrude is her name.' He held his hands out beseechingly. 'But I beg you, Sir Richard. Please say naught about me telling you their names.'

Richard eyed him sourly and gathered the things into his satchel. 'My man will call before long to remove the body. Meanwhile, do not let anyone touch it.'

Hubert had just jumped down from the wagon, leaving the two soldiers from the castle to guard the empty coffin under the heavy sacking. 'I have done as you ordered, my lord, and left Jane Henshaw's body in a cell. Is the summoner dead as the coroner's clerk Basil of Darrington said?'

Richard drew him down the street, out of the hearing of the men on the wagon. 'He is,' he said in a hushed voice. 'Murdered as well, but I have said nothing to the landlord. I need you to do exactly the same as you did with Jane the Healer's body.'

'Was he stabbed, too?' Hubert asked softly, keeping his face expressionless lest anyone should be alerted.

'No, he was knocked out, bound and then choked by having a ball of parchment stuffed down his windpipe. Then it was made to look as if he had died from apoplexy. That is what Barrowman the landlord thinks, and that is how it should remain until I have investigated and have a clearer picture in my mind.'

Hubert nodded. 'You may be interested to know that I saw that pilgrim that was robbed in Wakefield. Timothy of Halifax is his name. He was coming up the Micklegate as we were coming back down from the castle after arranging a cell for the girl's body. I hailed him and got down from the wagon. He stared at me for a moment, then recognised me.'

'He saw you? His vision was poor in my court.'

'Aye, my lord. That was what surprised me, but he told me that his sight had been restored after he had bathed his eyes in holy water that had been placed on what he called "blessed Thomas's tomb in the Priory Church."' Hubert gave a half smile. 'The truth is, though, I'm not sure he recognised my face, more he knew my voice. He still blinked a lot and his eyes were red, but that may have been from drinking. He was staggering a bit as he walked and needed that staff of his.'

'So he was happy?'

Hubert shook his head. 'He was not, my lord. He was talking loudly, shouting out at times about seeing sinners.'

'So he was drunk?'

'Aye, my lord. He admitted that he was. He told me that he had been overjoyed at getting his sight back after visiting the priory so he had sought to celebrate in a bawdy house. After being satisfied, he had bought and drunk two flagons of ale and some mead, more drink than he was used to. He was rubbing his eyes all the time he was telling me this and then he started blubbing about being sorry that he had sinned. That's when he started shouting out and drew folks' attention. He said that now his eyes were clearer, he saw sinners all around him — evil people who did not belong in Pontefract.'

'Were people laughing at him?'

'No, sir. It was like when you hear folks calling out in a market, like that tooth-puller in Wakefield. He was drawing attention to himself and folk wanted to hear what he had seen. Lots of folk had seen him about the town and knew him for a pilgrim. They wanted to know what evil he had seen. He just kept on about having seen evil folk, sinners, and then he said he's been cursed.'

'Cursed?' Richard repeated, his interest piqued.

'Yes, my lord. He said he thought that instead of receiving a miracle, perhaps he had been cursed, because he had been offended by what he had seen. By who he had seen.'

'Did he say more?'

'I don't know, Sir Richard. He was drawing more of a crowd than I thought was healthy, especially since I had a coffin on the wagon. I thought it would be best for me to come hither to the Pikestaff and collect the summoner's body, like you told me to.'

Richard patted Hubert on the shoulder. 'You acted correctly. Now go and deal with the summoner's body. But before you go, did Timothy of Halifax say which bawdy house he went to?'

'He did, Sir Richard. He said he had been told that it was the best in Pontefract and the girls were skilled and not unpleasing to the eye. Perhaps they were making a jest about his sight, or about the miracle he claimed to have had. He said it was run by a man called Bardolph.'

'Strangely, that is where the investigation takes me next. After you have placed the summoner in a dungeon cell and locked it, come meet me at the bawdy house. If I have left by that time, then go to Sir Nigel Fairfax's house, which is beyond the Corn Market. I must see how the coroner is faring and then I must investigate the death of Perkin Cratwell, the executioner.'

Richard found the building that Harald Barrowman had directed him to in one of the backstreets behind Salter's Row. The scent of spices hung heavy in the air, which was a momentary solace to his nostrils after having smelled the corruption of murdered bodies twice that day.

He crossed to the door and thumped on it with his gauntleted fist. Some moments later, a heavy grille slid open and a rodent-faced man looked out.

'You are Bardolph, I take it?' Richard asked. 'I am Sir Richard Lee, Circuit Judge of the King's Northern Realm and Judge of the Manor of Wakefield Court. I am investigating certain cases for Sir Nigel Fairfax the coroner, and I need to talk to you and to some of your — er — women.'

Bardolph looked startled. 'At once, sir.' He closed the grille, unbolted the door and threw it open to admit Richard. 'Is it about Jane Henshaw that you have come, sir?'

'What do you know of Jane Henshaw, Master Bardolph?' Richard asked sternly.

The brothelkeeper grimaced. 'A terrible thing to have happened, sir. Her being taken ill like that. It's the curse, I think.'

'What curse is that, Master Bardolph?' Richard asked.

The brothelkeeper looked perplexed. 'Why, the one that the whole town is talking about. The one that St Thomas of Lancaster made before he had his head cut off.'

'And how do you account for it being responsible for Jane Henshaw's illness? As I have heard it, the curse was made against the King, his chamberlain, Hugh le Despenser and the nobles present at his trial.'

'Ah, I am just saying what folks are talking about, sir. They talk of another curse made over in Carlisle.'

Interesting, the whole town is talking about these curses, Richard thought. 'I have not come to talk about Jane Henshaw,' he said pointedly.

Bardolph touched his forehead with a finger. 'Excuse my prattle, Sir Richard. Please, come through to my counting room. I have a fire lit and hot broth in the pot. Or wine, sir. I have wine.'

'I have heard that your wine is good, but I am not thirsty.'

Disappointment flashed across Bardolph's face as he wiped the chair next to the fire with his hand and gestured for Richard to be seated. 'Might I ask who told you about my wine, Sir Richard?'

'A pilgrim by the name of Timothy of Halifax.'

Bardolph beamed. 'Oh yes, a good man who had received a miracle at the priory. He had been blind, but now his vision has been cleared. He was in very good cheer.'

'He drank wine here?'

'Two flagons, sir, and then some mead. And he was entertained by one of our ladies.' He closed his eyes as if trying to remember. 'Ah yes, it was Marigold. He wanted a gentle lady, and she is that, sir.'

'I will speak with her, but first, I need to know how well did you know Simon of Holderness?'

'Did know him, Sir Richard? Why have you used the word *did*?'

'He is dead. He was found in his bed this day.'

Bardolph was visibly shocked. 'He was a customer on many of his visits, sir. He liked to relax with female company.'

'You know what he did for a living?'

'Aye, sir. He was a summoner. A good one, by all accounts. He certainly was not short of coin.'

Richard wiped some invisible dust from the knee of his breeches and went on casually. 'I am told that you and your women had an arrangement with him. He promised freedom from summonsing in return for free services. And I am also told that you and your women advised him on who were sinners and possible targets for summonses. He bragged that he would extort money from them in return for not issuing summonses to attend the Church Court.'

The brothelkeeper's cheeks glowed and his eyes widened in anger. 'What rogue would say such a thing, sir? It is not —'

Richard held up a hand. 'Don't deny this, Master Bardolph. I have no time to waste. Unless you wish to be charged with crimes and have this establishment closed down, you will answer me honestly. Do you understand?'

Bardolph swallowed hard and nodded. 'He was a villain and a sinner, sir. I ... I did not like doing...'

'You had an arrangement and you passed on names,' Richard stated, interrupting him. From the summoner's satchel, he drew out a piece of parchment and writing equipment. 'I want names and addresses, the misdemeanours these people were accused of and whether they were summonsed or whether they paid him bribes.'

Bardolph reeled off information about several people whose names he personally had supplied the summoner with. Like Harald Barrowman, he too pleaded that his name should not be given to any of them. And once again, Richard made no promise.

'Now I will see Marigold. I have several questions that I need to ask her about Timothy of Halifax.'

Marigold was a young woman of around twenty years. She was nervous about having to speak to a judge, but eager to answer as fully as she could. Richard saw her on her own after sending Bardolph out of his counting room.

'He was a strange little man, sir. So happy to be seeing, he said, although he stumbled and bumped into the cot. And he was pleased with me, sir. He gave me some extra coin. You won't tell Bardolph, though, will you, sir?'

So the pilgrim's sight does not seem to have been as miraculously cleared as he claimed. 'And he was quite happy when he left? Not angry, not talking about things he was able to see?'

Marigold looked puzzled. She shook her head. 'He was happy, sir. I believe he drank a lot of wine afterwards, but Bardolph will know about that better than me.'

Next, Richard called for Gertrude. Unlike Marigold, she showed few nerves and did not seem overawed by a judge. Accordingly, Richard deemed it apt to be forthright with her, as he had been with Bardolph. 'So, Gertrude, I will come straight to the point as I need to have answers and only honest answers. Simon of Holderness, the summoner, is dead and I need to know about the things he talked with you about.'

'Only what he talked about, Sir Richard?' she replied brazenly.

The strumpet seems neither sorrowful nor surprised, he thought. 'Had you heard about his death?'

She shook her head and shoved out her lower lip. 'First I heard about it was when Bardolph called me to see you, sir.'

'Are you not surprised?'

Again she shook her head indifferently. 'He was vigorous enough when he was with me, but he was not the healthiest of men. He had skin trouble and smelled a bit, but who can say?' She let out a short laugh. 'I am hardly an apothecary or surgeon.'

Richard decided not to rebuke her for impertinence. 'Did he have any enemies?'

'He was a summoner. There would be lots of folk that hated him. But why do you ask that, sir? Bardolph told me he died in his bed?'

Richard nodded. 'And so he did. I want to know the sort of things you told him. Bardolph told me that you passed on information about some of your customers.'

She eyed him warily. 'You won't go telling folks what I tell you, will you, sir? I mean, I have to keep men happy and don't want any of my customers to come here thinking they can give me a lesson to keep my mouth shut.'

She is clever, this one. 'No, I only need to know who you gave him information about.'

She visibly relaxed and gave him a number of names and the reasons why the summoner might wish to investigate or summons them.

'Was he an honest fellow, Gertrude?'

She giggled. 'Like a lot of us, he did what he did to make a living. He wasn't no saint, sir. He told me a lot about what he did. Men do that, talk to me when they lie there afterwards. A whore like me is everyone's friend, especially when I tells them they can trust me.'

'Do they all tell you secrets?'

She laughed again. 'No, sir. There are those that have secrets and they keep them to themselves. Like that one Simon was really interested in last time he visited me. He was some sort of holy man that didn't want anyone to know who he was. He always wore his gugel hood, even when he was having his way with me. I knew not to try to see his face, but I slipped my hand under his hood to stroke his head and I felt his tonsure. It was recently shaved and all stubbly.'

Could this be the same fellow they said had been to see Jane the Healer? Richard thought. 'Could he have been a friar, Gertrude?'

'A friar, a monk, anyone in the Church. But he had an accent and wasn't from around here. I can always tell when someone tries to change their voice. Simon, he liked to be a bit rough, but this one liked to hurt me and made sure that I showed it.' She gave him details as he pressed her.

'Did he have any really distinguishing features?'

'I told you, Sir Richard. He went to pains not to let me see overmuch of him. I never felt comfortable when he came. He only wanted me, so I made sure I didn't do anything to upset him.'

Richard wrote some further notes then sat back and stroked the end barbs of the quill. 'Bardolph informs me that Perkin Cratwell was also a customer of yours. Tell me about him.'

Gertrude shivered and held her hands up as if to somehow hold back the memories of the executioner. 'What ... what would you like to know about him, Sir Richard?'

'What sort of man was he? Was he rough like the man you just told me about? Or like Simon the Summoner?'

'He was a big man, sir. A strong man, as you would imagine. It may surprise you to know it, him being a torturer and an executioner, but he didn't like to hurt me. He was one of those that liked me to hurt him. I had to slap his buttocks until he would weep. Not real tears, of course, but he'd weep and then I had to give him a cuddle before he took his way the same as the rest.'

'Did he pay you well?'

She shook her head. 'He was one that had to be given special treatment.'

'You mean because he had the right of havage?'

She nodded. 'I know he didn't have that right in bawdy houses, but who in Pontefract would argue with him? Everyone let him have whatever he wanted.' She pouted in mock self-pity. 'Unfortunately, he always wanted me. He liked to tell me about his collections.'

'Collections of what?'

'Of clothes and things from those he had executed. Shirts, belts, rings. And about his ropes. He used a new one for every hanging.' She shivered at the thought. 'He was especially proud of the ones he had used on nobles.'

Richard made a note about this. 'Were you surprised to hear that he committed self-murder by hanging?'

She returned his look with narrowed eyes. 'I was, Sir Richard.'

'Did he seem melancholic to you?'

The bawd shook her head emphatically. 'He was not, sir. He was a lonely man, I think, on account of people keeping their distance from him. I think he had a lot of guilt, which could be why he wanted me to hit him, then cuddle him like a mother does to say that it will be all right.' She shivered again. 'I didn't like him myself. He made my skin crawl, but I think it was because of all the blood he had on his hands. Yet for all that, I am sure that he wasn't unhappy.'

'Why do you think he would hang himself, then?'

She suddenly made the sign of the cross over her heart. 'I think it was one of the curses, Sir Richard.'

Sir Richard left the bawdy house, made his way back to the Corn Market and headed for Sir Nigel Fairfax the coroner's large two-storey house. Banging on the door, he was admitted by a servant, who swiftly scuttled away and came back after a few moments with Basil of Darrington.

'I have seen and dealt with the two deaths,' Richard told him. 'I will consult with Sir Nigel about them when he is well enough. How is he now?'

Basil of Darrington shook his head and wrung his hands. 'He is abed and Doctor Jessop is seeing him now, Sir Richard. He has just bled him two pints.'

Richard put a hand on the man's arm. 'Before you take me to him, tell me if anything was kept belonging to Perkin Cratwell the executioner before he was buried.'

'Only his leather hood and the rope he hanged himself with, Sir Richard.'

'Are they here?'

Basil of Darrington nodded. 'They are in a chest in Sir Nigel's office.'

'Show me,' said Richard.

In the office, the clerk opened a large chest and pointed to a rope, still with its noose, and a leather hood with two eyeholes. Richard picked up the rope and sniffed distastefully. 'It smells horrible, as does his hood. I will take them to the castle when I am done here. We will say nothing yet to Sir Nigel if he is so ill. I am investigating all of his cases now.'

The clerk bowed and led the way up a creaking staircase to a chamber. Inside, a tall figure with a long grey beard, dressed in a grey robe, was standing over a gaunt-looking man lying in the bed. The patient was bathed in perspiration and was shivering. A younger man, obviously the physician's assistant, was wiping blood from a fleche and other bloodletting instruments and getting ready to put them away in a small portable medical chest on a bench beside a metal bowl full of dark red blood.

'What is the meaning of this?' snapped the tall man at Basil. 'I am treating a patient and said I was not to be disturbed.'

'I am Sir Richard Lee, Circuit Judge to His Majesty's Northern Realm,' Richard said coldly, taking an instant dislike to the physician. 'I have come to see my colleague, Sir Nigel, on whose behalf I have been working this day.'

'And I am Doctor Geoffrey Jessop, Sir Nigel's physician,' returned the other with a harrumph of displeasure. 'My patient has been treated and needs rest after his bloodletting.'

Sir Nigel was breathing with some difficulty, but his eyes still looked remarkably clear. He nodded weakly. 'Welcome ... Sir Richard,' he stuttered.

'I will not tire Sir Nigel,' Richard said. 'So if you have to go, Doctor Jessop —'

The physician gave him a sour look. 'I do have to see another patient, but I need to return later to let some more blood from Sir Nigel's other arm.'

'You are a bloodletting enthusiast, I understand, Doctor Jessop,' said Richard. 'I am staying at Pontefract Castle and saw Sir Clifford this morning.'

'I do not discuss my patients, but I will tell you this. Sir Nigel has an excess of blood and is of a sanguine disposition. This can cause blood to stagnate and cause paralysis from apoplexy. The treatment for his paralysis is to remove the excess offending humour, which is the blood.'

Richard nodded and stood aside. 'Ah, the Doctrine of Humours. Do not let me detain you, Doctor Jessop.'

'I shall return in two hours, Sir Nigel,' the physician said with a bow to his patient. He snapped his fingers at his young assistant and flounced heavily from the chamber. 'Good day, sir.'

Richard sat by the bed as Basil of Darrington followed the physician to show him out. 'Can you move your limbs, Sir Nigel?' he asked the coroner concernedly.

'I ... can ... barely breathe.'

'Has this been sudden, Sir Nigel?'

'Two ... three days. I feel ... so sick. Doctor ... Jessop says I must ... eat.'

'Have you a good cook?' Richard asked with a smile.

The coroner attempted to return the smile. 'He's good, but uses ... too much ... spice.'

'And what has your cook been giving you lately?'

'Quails. I … am … partial to them. Now I am … too sick.'

He is indeed unwell, yet his mind is not as affected as his body. 'There is no need to speak, Sir Nigel. Let me talk and you just listen. I have investigated these two deaths today, and I have grave concerns.'

Over the next quarter of an hour, Richard told the coroner of his findings, omitting any mention about Perkin Cratwell. He decided that he would talk about him later, when and if the coroner recovered.

Footsteps on the creaking wooden stairs caused him to look round as the door opened and Basil of Darrington came in. 'May I assist you, Sir Richard?'

'Yes, I would like to see your cook.'

The clerk looked puzzled. 'I am afraid that you can't, Sir Richard. He has packed his things and gone. Without a word.'

Richard merely nodded, then turned to look down at the coroner. 'Sir Nigel, my man will be here soon. With your permission, I am going to take you from here.'

The coroner continued to breathe heavily. 'I … fear it may be … too late. I am … dying.'

I fear that is the case, too, Richard thought. *Yet there is still hope.*

Hubert arrived a short while later with the wagon and a single soldier. Under Richard's instructions, they carried Sir Nigel downstairs and lifted him onto the wagon. Richard climbed up and put the summoner's satchel and the other bag containing Perkin Cratwell's things under the bench.

'Are we returning to the castle, my lord?'

'No. Take us to St Mary Magdalene's Hospital with all good speed.'

As the two horses drew the wagon through the streets of

Pontefract, many people stopped to watch its progress. At the sight of the coroner wrapped in blankets, there were many mutterings about curses, sorcery and witchcraft. Many people made the sign of the cross or clutched personal charms or talismans.

Among the crowd was a figure wearing a gugel hood pulled down over the upper part of the face. This person had killed twice and would have no hesitation about doing so again, even taking the life of the King's own Circuit Judge if there was any risk that their plans could be discovered.

Mother Cecilia was surprised when the coroner was unceremoniously carried into the hospital, but she sent for Sister Esmeralda after Richard introduced himself and explained the situation.

'How long has Sir Nigel been ill?' Sister Esmeralda asked a few minutes later as she and Richard stood over the bed upon which the coroner had been laid.

'Three days or so.'

'With your permission, Sir Nigel,' she said, gently examining his limbs.

'Doctor Jessop has been letting his blood,' Richard explained. 'He said that Sir Nigel was of a sanguine disposition and had too much blood. I know something of the Doctrine of Humours, yet I am not convinced. I think that the doctor probably bleeds most of his patients.'

Sister Esmeralda nodded noncommittally. She addressed Sir Nigel, who was breathing with difficulty and looking anxiously at her. 'Did this paralysis affect one side of your body first, Sir Nigel?'

The coroner shook his head. 'It began ... in both feet ... and then slowly ... moved up. Now ... can't breathe.'

Sister Esmeralda leaned closer to him and sniffed his breath. She said nothing, but Richard saw that she had winced.

'What is your opinion, Sister Esmeralda?' he asked.

Sister Esmeralda shook her head and touched Sir Nigel's hand. 'You are aware of what we are saying, are you not, Sir Nigel?'

The coroner nodded and weakly turned his hand to grasp the nun's fingers.

'I thought so,' she went on, giving the coroner a smile. 'Your mind is sharp, despite your body being so weak. This makes me believe that this is not a case of apoplexy, but of poisoning.' She squeezed Sir Nigel's hand. 'Someone has given you hemlock. I can smell its malevolent odour on your breath. It causes this type of creeping paralysis that causes weakness of all the muscles until the breathing ones that work the lungs stop working. We need to get it out of your system.'

'With more bloodletting?' Richard asked cautiously.

'No, Sir Richard. I have two bezoar stones, one taken from the stomach of a goat and the other from a sheep. I will immerse them in wine and make some decoctions of liquorice, rhubarb and theriac to purge his system. I will also apply various unguents to Sir Nigel's feet to draw out the poison.' She looked at the coroner and then at Richard and added, 'And I will pray for his recovery.'

CHAPTER NINE

When Richard and Hubert returned to the castle later that day, Richard summoned Martin of Helmsley and instructed him to show him where Perkin Cratwell had lived. He was shown to a small chamber above the postern gate.

'Did you know him well?' Richard asked the page as he surveyed the room with its pallet bed, two stools, a small table upon which was a half-used tallow candle, an empty jug and a mug. Side by side against the wall were three large chests.

'Not well, Sir Richard. I saw him about the castle and Pontefract often, but he had no position in the castle, so he came and went as he pleased.'

'He had free access to the kitchens?'

'Yes, my lord. And to the cellar and brewhouse. None of the servants would dare challenge him.'

'You knew what he did?'

Martin of Helmsley flushed. 'We all did, Sir Richard, but we were forbidden to ask him anything about it.' He gritted his teeth. 'I would not want to know too much, my lord.'

'Have any of his possessions been touched?'

'No, Sir Richard. Sir Clifford had not given any instructions; so as far as I know, no one has been inside this chamber since he died.'

'You know how he died?' Richard asked casually.

The page visibly shuddered. 'He ... he hanged himself, my lord.'

'And what is the talk among the servants and soldiers in the castle? Why did he do that?'

'We ... we think it was to do with the curse, my lord.'

Richard nodded. 'That will do, Martin. I will see myself out.'

When the page departed, Richard set about examining the chests. The first contained several changes of clothes and an assortment of personal items. As Richard hoped, the second contained his collections of items of clothing, handkerchiefs, several Bibles and a number of crosses of various materials. Clearly they were the keepsakes or trophies he had taken to mark the many executions he had performed. He took them out one by one and laid them on the bed so that he could examine them more closely. Without written notes on them, for he imagined that the executioner could not write, he was unable to identify many as belonging to individuals, apart from those Bibles which had been inscribed, or handkerchiefs that had been embroidered with a family crest.

As he went through them, he noticed that some of the things were bloodstained. Others had strands or locks of hair tied to them. The Bibles also had snippets laid inside them. Here, he had no doubt, was Perkin Cratwell's personal system for identifying each one of the sudden deaths he had caused. Or indeed, some of the prolonged executions.

A large wooden board inside the second chest had a hole in it so that it could be lifted out. And there Richard found two shirts he had suspected he might find. One had the crest of the House of Lancaster embroidered upon it, the other that of what he presumed was the coat of arms of the Earl of Carlisle.

So Perkin Cratwell despatched both earls, he mused to himself.

Turning his attention to the third chest, he found that it contained the collection of ropes that Gertrude the bawd had told him existed. As with the other trophy items, these all had human hair tied round them.

He counted sixty-three ropes. It felt unnerving handling these individual tools of death. He sniffed them all.

Very interesting; there is no particular smell other than of rope, he mused.

But the actual nooses interested him most.

At supper with Sir Clifford and Lady Justina in the small hall of the pre-kitchen tower, which was directly above the bakehouse and was one of the warmest places in the whole castle, Richard informed the constable of his investigations on behalf of Sir Nigel Fairfax, albeit without telling him that he had reached any conclusions. Sir Clifford was already aware that the bodies of Simon of Holderness and Jane Henshaw had been placed in the dungeon. Richard told him that he was keeping the bodies in the castle until he held an inquest, when he would review all the witness statements.

'I also called upon Sir Nigel and found that his condition had deteriorated, so I took him to be looked after by the nuns at St Mary Magdalene's Hospital.'

Sir Clifford was in the process of raising a piece of roasted duck to his mouth, but stopped and stared in surprise. 'But I understood that Doctor Jessop was treating him?'

'He was letting his blood, that is correct.'

Lady Justina bit her lip. 'I fear that the good doctor will be upset, Sir Richard.'

Richard raised his hands matter-of-factly. 'He will have learned already, as he was going to call again to remove more blood.'

Sir Clifford harrumphed. 'He is a very learned doctor, and he has been treating me since the attack on my person. He has almost healed my leg, and I am slowly regaining my strength.'

'He said it would be a slow process,' Lady Justina added.

Richard picked up his goblet and sipped his wine. 'I am glad that you are recovering so well, Sir Clifford. But as for Sir

Nigel, let me just say that he deteriorated quickly after Doctor Jessop left, and I felt that I had to take him most urgently for further care.' *Besides which*, he thought, *I have seen men bleed to death on the battlefield. I think his bloodletting is more likely to kill than cure. So let the good doctor be upset.*

By the light of four candles in his chamber that evening, Richard sat examining the contents of the summoner's satchel in more detail. Sitting on a stool on the other side of the table, Hubert polished his dagger and his sword.

Richard placed the notes that he had made on one side of the table along with Simon of Holderness's writing equipment, noting that although not a clerk, the summoner had looked after his implements. Taking out all of the parchment writs, he placed them in various piles. First were those written in a single scholarly hand and signed by Walter Lydford, Dean of St Salvator's Church and Commissary General of the York Consistory Court. Next were several others also signed by the dean, but without names written in. Lastly a pile with names written in by another, less scholarly, hand.

Richard sat back for a moment and tapped the table with his fingers.

'Are you troubled by something, my lord?' Hubert asked.

'Not troubled as much as intrigued, Hubert. It seems that the summoner was sent to Pontefract tasked with summonsing specific named individuals.' He reached for the first pile and flicked through them. 'Here is a writ made out for Jane Henshaw, known as Jane the Healer, summonsed for blasphemy and charlatanry.'

'News of her must have reached York and upset the Archdeacon, my lord.'

'Or the Archdeacon's assistant, the Dean of St Salvator's.'

'But why blasphemy?'

Richard shrugged. 'It may be because the Church wants to supress the cult of Thomas of Lancaster and any who proclaim him in any way to be saintly.' He thumbed through the next few writs. 'And here are eight named men, summonsed for attacking the Priory of St John a few weeks ago. That would be when the constable was attacked and the two soldiers were killed.' He flicked through more. 'And these others, which were all to be served.' He picked up the second pile. 'These were obviously writs to be used at the summoner's discretion. I take it from this that he was effectively given free licence to summons anyone that he considered guilty of misdemeanours according to ecclesiastic law. That is actually a broad sweep, for so many things are considered immoral behaviour.'

Richard turned his attention to the last pile on top of which was the parchment he had removed from the summoner's throat. It was creased from being bundled up, but he had wiped it clean and smoothed it out as best he could. 'This is a blank writ,' he said, lifting it up. 'I think it was probably used by the murderer because it was a blank one. Either that or it was randomly picked up.' He placed it on the table and held up the next. 'This second parchment is blank and has a list of names, several of which have been crossed out. Three of the ones crossed out are named on writs made out by the Ecclesiastical Court clerk. I think these are people from whom he had taken bribes to say that he could not summons them. Similarly, there are crossed out names that accord with writs that he had filled in himself.'

'The summoner was a devious, thieving rogue, it seems, my lord.'

'Other names have simply been ticked, and I find no summonses. It is likely that these were ones that he had actually issued with summonses. All in all, it looks as if he was starting to issue summonses, he was collecting bribes and he was intending to extort others with spurious summonses.'

'So the murderer could be one of these names?'

'Indeed he might, although according to Harald Barrowman, the landlord of the Pikestaff Inn, the pilgrim who stayed the night and who mysteriously disappeared had only one leg. When you go over to the kitchens for breakfast tomorrow, I want you to ask if there are any one-legged men in Pontefract.'

'I shall be discreet in my asking, my lord.'

'Also, tomorrow I want you to begin searching these people out. But in particular I want you to question these three named individuals whose names are crossed off the list. I want to know what they were being summonsed for and what they gave the summoner to spare them an appearance in the Church Court.'

'May I use persuasion, my lord?'

'Discretion, Hubert,' Richard said archly. 'We are the law and must act lawfully.'

'You still look concerned, my lord.'

Richard smiled. 'Yes, it is this last parchment that puzzles me most. It seems to be a mixture of Latin legal terms and Latin doggerel. Written in a shakier hand than his other lists.'

Hubert frowned as he stood and went round the table to look over Richard's shoulder. 'I am grateful that you taught me reading, my lord, but this Latin is beyond me.'

Richard bit his lip pensively. 'Some of these entries are old and the ink has faded. This one, "*in flagrante delicto*", means "blazing" — essentially caught in the act. I see that he has used that on some summonses. This one, "*feme covert*", means a married woman. He will have used that in cases of adultery. "*Ejusdem generis*" means of the same sort or same class. He'd use that if citing similar misdemeanours. "*Jus ad rem*" would mean a right thing to do. "*Mala prohibita*" is just a prohibited wrong, and "*non compos mentis*" is "not of sound mind", which would be a reasonable defence for many things.' He ran his finger down. 'Just about twenty lines of law terms, as if he used them to refresh his memory to appear knowledgeable about Latin legal terms. But then there are these five lines in fresh ink and the very last of them with a shaky hand. I imagine that last line was written at a later time, although all are relatively recent.' He read them out loud: '*Ab m n ex swin; fac pec pon; pat ex nec alc; dom puel; ego peric.*'

'Is it Latin, my lord? Maybe the shaky hand was from drinking. Could it all be just drunken doggerel?'

Richard shrugged. 'Possibly. Yet I think it is Latin doggerel, for they are not proper words. Unless they are abbreviations. In that case, the last two lines could be "*domum puellae*" and "*ego periculum.*"'

'I am no wiser, my lord.'

'If I am right, they mean "the girl's house" and "I am in danger."'

Richard looked up at Hubert. 'Perhaps his hand shook when he wrote that last line because he somehow realised that he was in danger of being murdered.'

The next morning, armed with two lanterns, Hubert and Richard went down to the castle dungeon, reached via a long flight of stone steps leading down from a basement in the keep. As directed, Hubert had retained the keys to the cells in which the bodies had been placed in their rough wooden coffins.

'Did you find out about any one-legged people in the town?' Richard asked.

'There is only one that the cooks and a few of the servants who visit the town regularly know of, Sir Richard. He is a leper the locals call Lazarus One Leg. He lives at the Lazar House near St Mary Magdalene's Hospital. He is occasionally seen begging on the Gillygate or at the crossroads coming into town from the south.'

'I shall make it my business to visit the Lazar House when I next go to see Sir Nigel at St Mary Magdalene's Hospital,' Richard replied.

Hubert unlocked the cell containing the coffin of the summoner. While Hubert held the lantern aloft, Richard described his findings on the corpse of Simon of Holderness.

'Whoever did this knew precisely what they were doing, Hubert. They wanted to leave no trace of the violent death and did not expect that the parchment would be discovered. It was only when I smelled his breath that I thought I could detect the musty odour of parchment, and that made me look and then fish it out with one of the summoner's quills.'

'Shall we look at Jane Henshaw's body, too, my lord?'

'In a moment, Hubert. I wanted you to be familiar with the summoner's cause of death, just as you are already with the girl's. It will be important to have the bodies brought in when we hold the inquest on their deaths. I want the girl's face to be covered and for both to have shrouds over their clothes.'

'Shall I get the servants to do this, my lord?'

'No, I want you alone to do this, because there is something that I want you to do before they are brought in.'

'Whatever you wish, my lord.'

'Come, let us see the girl's body and I will explain. Then afterwards I want you to track down those three people whose names were crossed off the summoner's list of writs to be served. As for myself, I must see the headborough and then I will look for this mysterious one-legged pilgrim or the elusive friar.'

Richard rode down the wide Micklegate from the castle and found the house belonging to Rupert Shenley, the headborough, behind Finkle Street. It was set back from the road by a small field where a flock of sheep were free to graze. The headborough was in his office dealing with various business matters, but when Mistress Bernice tapped upon the door to inform him that Sir Richard had come to visit, he quickly came and left his clerk to carry on until he returned.

'Sir Richard, you do us honour in visiting,' he said, as Richard rose from the settle when he came in. 'I was just arranging a consignment of wool to go east to Hull. How may I serve you?'

'It is an official call rather than a social one, I am afraid,' said Richard. 'I came to ask you as the headborough to put out a proclamation. I am acting on behalf of Sir Nigel Fairfax the coroner, who has been taken ill. I will be holding an inquest into the deaths of Jane Henshaw and of Simon of Holderness, a Summoner from the York Consistory Court.'

Bernice Shenley gasped. 'Such a shame, the poor girl being taken ill so suddenly. But she died; that is tragic.'

Rupert Shenley put a comforting hand on her shoulder. 'I heard about her death yesterday. The town is full of gossip, I am afraid to say. It has increased the talk about the two curses, made by Thomas the Earl of Lancaster and Sir Andrew Harclay, the Earl of Carlisle. What do you think, Sir Richard? Could there be two curses, and could one work against the other?'

'I have no doubt that there were two curses made, Master Shenley, but whether there is anything in them is another matter. I am not convinced that mere words can have a material effect in the real world.'

The headborough shrugged his shoulders. 'And yet the people of Pontefract clearly think differently. As I go about, I hear talk all the time about blessed Thomas, as he is now referred to, or about miracles that have been happening at his tomb and then again after people have seen Jane Henshaw and had ailments cured.'

'I believe such things are possible, Sir Richard,' said Mistress Shenley. 'The Lord works in so many ways.'

'Is there a problem with the summoner's death, Sir Richard?' the headborough asked.

'It was a sudden death, and since Sir Nigel Fairfax is unwell and cannot investigate it, I will hold the inquest. So, can I leave it to you to make the proclamation and ensure that the inquest is attended? It is everyone's duty to come, and from them I shall appoint at random twelve men of the jury.'

'Will you hold it in the Court House, Sir Richard? And when will it be?'

'The Court House at the eleventh hour tomorrow.'

From the headborough's house Richard journeyed past the Monk's Hill where Thomas of Lancaster had been executed and then past St John's Priory. He crossed the bridge over the town ditch as the road gently climbed higher. There were by this time many carts and wagons upon the road and still more travellers on donkeys or on foot, often herding small numbers of beasts either to or from Pontefract.

About a mile from Pontefract he saw the Stump Cross by the side of the road. It was a twelve-foot-high stone cross that marked the outer boundary of the borough. Richard dismounted and stood inspecting it. Upon its front was an elaborate carving of a man on horseback and on the reverse a seated figure, although whether it was a king or a bishop he could not determine. Yet it was not that which he wanted to see. It was the crossbar itself, where Perkin Cratwell had hanged himself and was found in the morning by a troupe of wandering actors. *Actors that had disappeared as if they had never been there*, Richard mused.

Looking about the foot of the cross, he was aware of the stench of dung and saw little dribbles of it in the mud. Bending and sniffing, it was clear that it was not just ordinary animal dung, but night soil. Looking upwards at the crosspiece, he saw marks where undoubtedly a rope had been tied. On further inspection, he could see a smear of dung.

So, Perkin Cratwell, the story is that you came here one night in a fit of melancholy, either the result of an imbalance in your humours, or because of a curse upon you. You then ended your life by hanging yourself.

'No, it will not do,' Richard said out loud to himself. *Where is the stone or whatever you used to stand on? If you came on a donkey, where did it go? And why did the rope you hanged yourself with stink of night soil, just as there are dribbles of it by the cross? The answer is simple. You didn't hang yourself. I think you were already dead, brought here in a gong wagon in the dead of night.*

An hour later, Richard took the road south towards Darrington from the castle. He reached the familiar crossroads where one road led to St Mary Magdalene's Hospital and the other towards the Lazar House. Steeling himself, he turned his horse towards the Lazar House.

There was nothing bright about the high-walled enclosure. A figure of a penitent knight was cut into its grey stone, indicating the Order of St Lazarus of Jerusalem. The gates were closed and a bell rope hung down beside them. Richard dismounted and tethered his horse before pulling the bell several times. It took a few minutes before his call was answered and a wooden shutter in the gate was pulled open.

'Yes, my son, are you lost?' came a gentle voice from within.

'No, I am not lost. I am Sir Richard Lee, Sergeant-at-Law and the Circuit Judge of His Majesty's Northern Realm. I am acting on behalf of Sir Nigel Fairfax, who is ill at present.'

'I am Father Percival, Sir Richard. I am the prior of this house dedicated to St Lazarus of Jerusalem. And as you may see, I am afflicted by leprosy, as are we all, which is why our gates are closed. It is not that we are inhospitable.'

'I will not keep you long then, Father Percival. I am looking into a case and I have heard that you have someone living here called Lazarus One Leg. May I see him?'

The prior looked slightly crestfallen. 'It is a cruel name that people have called one of our house. His name is actually Brother Lucas. I will fetch him if you will wait here.'

Richard nodded, grateful that he was not admitted to the Lazarus House itself, for even though he knew it was unlikely that he would contract the disease, like most people he felt more comfortable keeping a distance.

The gates opened and the prior came out, helping a man on two crutches. He wore a grey gown with the hood up, partially covering his face, which was still visible and showed a collapsed nose and several sores. The hands that gripped the crutches were missing three digits and he balanced on one sandaled foot.

'Sir Richard would like a word with you, Lucas,' Father Percival said.

Richard gave an embarrassed smile. 'I merely need to check whether you have only one leg?'

Lucas reached down and grasped his gown, pulling it up to reveal that both legs were in fact present, but one was bent at a deformed knee. The foot was also deformed, and like his hands, was missing two digits. 'I have all four limbs, Sir Richard,' he said. 'People mistakenly think that we lepers lose hands, feet or whole limbs. The truth is we lose feelings, so we injure ourselves and we develop sores that can fester. My knee has become misshapen and fixed in this position, and my foot has had many such injuries. It may look as if I have one leg, but I still have the other; it just does not reach the ground and is hidden by my gown.'

Richard felt guilty for his own misunderstanding of the condition. Clearly, neither Father Percival nor Brother Lucas would have the strength to overpower Simon of Holderness, the summoner. 'I am truly sorry to have bothered you, Brother Lucas and Father Percival. But you have indeed been a great help to me.'

The two lepers watched him mount up and ride off along to the crossroads, where he went straight ahead towards St Mary Magdalene's Hospital.

'It felt good to have been of some use, Father Percival,' said Brother Lucas. 'It has been a long time since I heard anyone say that to me.'

The prior helped him retire inside, then closed the gates to once more shut the world out of their grey, unloved lives.

Mother Cecilia greeted Richard and took him to the chamber where Sister Esmeralda was looking after Sir Nigel.

'He sleeps,' Sister Esmeralda whispered, a smile on her lips.

Mother Cecilia smiled. 'She has been with him all the time, and this is the first time that he has not been struggling to breathe.'

'Bezoar stones are wondrous in their action at absorbing poisons,' Sister Esmeralda said softly. 'But I have made several different concoctions of liquorice and rhubarb as well as giving hourly theriac to purge it from him. I think it is working. Now he needs to sleep.'

'Will he regain the use of his limbs and be able to walk again?' Richard asked.

'That is up to God,' Mother Cecilia replied. 'That is also why Sister Esmeralda looks so exhausted. She has been praying all the time she has been treating him.'

'Then I will detain you no longer. But tell me, are there any monks or friars that you know of with only one leg?'

Both nuns shook their heads.

'Then I must next visit St Richard's Friary.'

Richard returned towards Pontefract, then turned off left through woodland until he came to the valley where St Richard's Friary stood. Surrounded by fields with grazing sheep, it had a low surrounding wall, and as its backdrop it had the cliff that Father Friar Alfred had told him about at the feast in celebration of the Stigmata of St Francis of Assisi. The friary had a central bell tower with wings on either side, one being the chapel and the other the kitchens. A chapter house with a quadrangle and cloister stood in front of it. To the west was a large cemetery with neatly tended graves and headstones.

Richard rode through the open gates and was met by a friar dressed in the white habit and black mantle of the Dominican order, who was carrying a bundle of logs towards the kitchens. He offered to take him to see Father Friar Alfred, who was praying in his cell.

'I am sorry to interrupt your prayers, Father Alfred,' Richard said as the older friar rose from his knees in front of his personal lectern, which had an open prayer book and a carved wooden crucifix atop it. 'I have been visiting Sir Nigel Fairfax, who has been taken ill and is being treated at St Mary Magdalene's Hospital.'

'I had heard that the coroner had been taken ill, my son. I hope that he is comfortable.'

'He seems to be in good hands,' Richard replied.

'We are all in God's hands, my son. Mortal hands may deliver physic, splint broken limbs or cut away warts, stones or cankers, but only God heals.'

'Are you not a believer in physic, Father?'

The friar smiled. 'I believe that the words and deeds are important, Sir Richard. Good will always be rewarded and evil will ultimately be overcome by God's goodness. As Friars of St Richard, we study the scriptures, pray and preach the word of the Lord. That is our mission, to go from here in pairs, along the different roads and find those who will listen to our preaching.'

'You go in pairs?' Richard repeated.

'Always, when we go preaching. We leave in pairs and are never far from one another. It is partly for safety and also to ensure that we can collect a gathering, rather like a shepherd and his dog.'

Richard nodded. 'You are a mendicant order, are you not? So you receive money when preaching?'

'We are. We have no property apart from that which has been given to us by charity. Our land was thus given and the cemetery that we tend is done for charity. We permit people to be buried here and in return we pray for their souls and tend their graves.'

'And the families donate to charity.'

Friar Alfred bowed his tonsured head in acknowledgement.

'How many of your order are there?'

'Including myself, we have fourteen brother friars.'

'Ever any more?'

'No, Sir Richard, but we are always open and willing to give any who call for it shelter and food.'

'Did you have a summoner visit you?'

'No, Sir Richard. We have no one who transgresses.'

'Or have you ever had any infirm people call on you? Anyone with a limb missing?'

'Not to my recollection. I wonder about your questioning, Sir Richard. Is there a reason for it?'

Outside, a bell rang several times.

'There is, but I may not tell you at this time. May I meet your friars?'

Friar Alfred smiled. 'You just heard the noon bell, calling us to sext, the third of the Little Hours when we will recite the divine office. Today, all of our order will be present. You are welcome to attend.'

Richard followed the friar to the church. Outside the door, Friar Alfred pointed to three foundation stones in the wall. 'Our friary is dedicated to three saints, not simply St Richard. When our founder Edmund de Lacy chose Pontefract to establish a friary in 1256, he dedicated it to St Richard, who had been his tutor before he became Bishop of Chichester. You can see fragments of his dedication on all three stones.'

Richard read it out: *To the honour of our Lady Mary, mother of God and Virgin, and of St Dominic, confessor, to whose brethren I assign this place, and also of St Richard, bishop and confessor, formerly my lord and dearest friend, I wishing to found a church in this place lay the first stone.*

Friar Alfred went on, 'Upon those words, the stone split in three, hence we have three foundations, each with part of the

171

dedication. It was taken as a sign of approval for having the three patron saints.'

He gestured for Richard to enter the church where the brother friars had already taken their places. Friar Alfred went to the lectern at the front and after a few words, began the recitation.

Richard watched as the friars bent their heads and joined in, before all eventually knelt in prayer. They varied in age from early twenties to near sixty years or more. Not one of them seemed robust enough to hold a man down and kill him. He looked at their heads. All showed growth of hair over their tonsured pates.

When the service was over, Richard watched the brother friars file out then asked Friar Alfred one more question. 'How often do your friars have their tonsures shaven?'

The friar looked puzzled. 'Once a month, when the barber from Pontefract calls. He should be here in about a week.'

Hubert had managed to track down all three of the men whose names had been crossed off the summoner's list. Each of them at first denied any knowledge of Simon of Holderness, but Hubert's blunt approach and physical presence and the guarantee of immunity from being summoned to the Consistory Court, which Richard had told him to give them, resulted in them divulging their misdeeds. One had stolen wine from church, another had slept with his brother's wife and the last admitted to poaching coneys on Sunday instead of going to church. They also told him how much they had paid the summoner to protect them from the Church Court.

He was returning to the castle along the Bondgate when he was accosted by a young serving woman. She came running towards him as he passed a mansion set well back from the road.

'Help, sir, I beg you. My mistress, Lady Elizabeth, has had a grievous shock.'

'Do you mistake me for a physician?' Hubert returned. 'I am no —'

'Please, sir, she is in distress and Sir Baldwin is not at home. She was in the garden getting greenery to take to All Saints' Church across the road, and she found it, sir. The dead man.' Without warning, the young woman turned and vomited.

Hubert waited helplessly until she had finished retching. Then she recovered herself and took a deep breath.

'It is a horrible sight, sir.'

Hubert quickly followed her around the back of the mansion and saw a lady leaning with her back against a wall of the building, sobbing and holding her hands over her face.

'I have brought a man, my lady,' the serving woman said.

Lady Elizabeth opened her eyes and with a look of horror pointed to a small hedge. 'In ... in there,' she said between sobs.

Hubert strode over to the hedge and found himself looking down at the body of the pilgrim, Timothy of Halifax. His hands were over his face and congealed blood caked the sides of his neck. As Hubert bent closer, he saw that a thumb was buried in each eye socket.

CHAPTER TEN

As he mounted his horse and retraced his way to the road, Richard saw a ledge cut into the cliff face, about twenty feet above the base of the cliff. A wooden staircase built against the cliff led to the ledge, where a wooden door and a window were visible.

'So this is where Peter the Hermit lives,' he said to himself, turning to approach the steps. He rode towards them, dismounted, tethered his horse and ascended the stairs.

The door was closed, but a bell hung by it.

In answer to its clang, he heard movement from within, then a voice called out. 'Be patient, whoever thou art, for I am old and I savour each moment, as should you.'

A few moments later, the door was unbolted and pulled open, and an old man of at least three score years with long, unkempt grey hair and a bushy, braided beard a foot long stood smiling at him. He was dressed in a simple, dusty robe and sandals made of rope. 'I hope you are not too troubled, young man,' he said, using both hands to stroke aside wisps of hair from his cheeks. Then he sniffed, causing the nostrils on his large snubbed nose to almost twitch. 'You don't happen to have brought any cheese, do you? An important man like you is surely bound to carry cheese.'

Slightly taken aback and bemused at the question, Richard hesitated a moment before apologetically replying in the negative.

'No matter, I assume that you have come to ask a question of Peter the Hermit, for I am he and you are standing there having found your way to my humble abode and place of worship. What question have you for me, my friend?'

Richard smiled in return. 'I am Sir Richard Lee, Circuit Judge to His Majesty, King Edward, and I am acting on behalf of Sir Nigel Fairfax. I have heard that you have visions. One vision in particular, that —'

To Richard's surprise, the hermit raised a hand, stood aside and bid him enter. When he stepped inside, he was amazed to see by the light from the window and from two small oil lamps in niches that Peter had hewn an altar from the sandstone rock and created a perfectly domed roof. Upon the altar was a simple wooden cross. On the walls Peter had carved depictions of biblical scenes, and on the floor in front of the altar was a single kneeler.

'When I am deep in prayer, I am often sent messages and images, or what you would call visions. Some are from angels, others from saints and a few are from God himself.'

'I hear that you had one such message about the girl, Jane Henshaw.'

'I did, and it came true.'

'Were you told that the archbishop would like to meet her?'

Peter the Hermit shook his head. 'The angel Michael who came to me only told me that a girl would have a vision and receive a gift from the blessed Thomas of Lancaster.'

Richard was aware of a strange sense of familiarity as he looked at the hermit standing before his rock-hewn altar. He glanced admiringly at the chamber walls and their carvings and pointed to one. 'Is that a representation of the angel Michael?'

The hermit smiled. 'It is exactly as he looks to me when he visits.'

'You have created a remarkable place to worship and live.'

'I am comfortable and have few needs. I have water in my well below, and people come and bring me food. The Lord provides for me.'

'You asked if I had a question for you, Peter the Hermit. Well, I have. It is simply this: did Perkin Cratwell commit self-murder?'

The hermit looked perplexed. 'I cannot answer that, Sir Richard. I have been given no message about this Perkin Cratwell. I am afraid that I do not know of him at all. Was he a worldly man?'

Richard nodded. 'He was until he departed this life. Now he is of the other world.'

Peter the Hermit bowed and made the sign of the cross over his heart. 'In that case, he will now know all the answers and will receive the rewards or the just deserts that he earned in this life.'

From the hermitage Richard rode to St John's Priory, again passing the Monk's Hill and the site of Thomas of Lancaster's execution with the large cross. Lots of people were gathered around it, praying or smearing themselves with earth or collecting soil in jars or other receptacles. As he passed by them, he also heard raised voices and saw some of the folk were bickering about things with jabbing of fingers, shaking of fists, but without actual fighting.

Feelings are running high and not everyone is here to venerate Lancaster, he thought.

He rode through the priory gates and was greeted by a monk who, after Richard had stated his purpose of seeing the prior and visiting the tomb of Thomas of Lancaster, offered to stable his horse and then fetch Prior Stephen.

Inside the Priory Church, pilgrims were taking turns to visit the tomb at the right-hand side of the high altar. The tomb was covered by a solid oblong block of honey-coloured stone, upon which a jug and a bowl of water had been placed on either side of the etched coat of arms of Thomas of Lancaster.

Light streamed through the beautiful stained glass of the church windows, dappling the floor and the stone tomb with an array of colours. Some women knelt before the tomb sobbing, while others prayed whilst stroking and even kissing the tomb.

Richard stood and watched for a while, observing two monks at the rear of the nave handing out small clay pots, for which pilgrims left offerings in a wooden bowl.

'Good day, Sir Richard,' came the prior's familiar voice behind him. 'I take it you have come to view the tomb of blessed Thomas for yourself.'

'I have, Prior Stephen. And to see the pilgrims and how they come in such numbers.'

'All are welcome,' replied the prior. He pointed to the Lazar window. 'Even our brothers and sisters from the Lazar House.'

'Yet they cannot enter the church?'

'I am afraid that I do not make the laws, Sir Richard.'

'And yet you have defied His Majesty's wishes and allow all to visit the tomb?'

'They were merely his wishes, not his commands, Sir Richard.'

'And Archbishop Melton was ordered by the King to suppress the pilgrimages and idolatry.'

Prior Stephen put his hands in his voluminous sleeves. 'We are of the Cluniac Order, Sir Richard. Our authority is the Abbey *La Charité-sur-Loire* in France, not the Archbishop of York. Besides, after the attack upon Sir Clifford, I called upon him at the castle and we agreed that for the sake of public order, it would be best to allow pilgrims to visit the tomb. Especially when they were gaining so much good and the miracles were happening.'

Richard nodded. He was already aware of this from the constable, but had wanted to hear it from the prior's lips. He also wanted to put him at his ease. 'Can we walk about the priory? There are other matters I wish to discuss.'

They left the church and walked through the chapter house and refectory to enter the large cloister that surrounded a central lawn. With its high arched roof, straw-covered floor and individual cubicles they passed several monks, writing and painting at desks.

'My monks have many daily tasks to perform,' Prior Stephen explained. 'At this time of day, when the light is good, these brothers are busy translating texts, these others in copying and illustrating manuscripts.'

'And beautifully they do it,' Richard remarked. 'And they do manual work, too?'

'Indeed, we have herds of cattle and sheep, fields to tend and all the work of a farm. As you probably already know, three brothers and two lay brothers also look after the sick in St Nicholas's Hospital behind All Saints' Church. But of course, it is *opus Dei*, the work of God that most concerns us. We have eight services a day and must pray, contemplate and study. We give our lives to spiritual matters.'

'How many monks are there here?'

'We have twenty, twenty-one including myself.'

'All are tonsured?'

Prior Stephen shook his head. 'Six are lay brothers, not yet taken into the Order.'

'And are all well? Does any have a limb missing?'

'Strange questions, Sir Richard,' the prior replied with a thin smile. 'No, thank the Lord, we are all well and able in body.'

'I come then to another matter. Have you had any dealings with a summoner called Simon of Holderness?'

'Ah!' Prior Stephen exclaimed. 'Has he been to consult you? I did indeed see him only a day or so ago. He claimed that two of my monks had committed simony and wanted to issue them with summonses. But I explained that they had not. They were freely giving samples of earth.'

'I saw two monks doing this in the church,' Richard stated.

'Quite so, and you would have seen that people made offerings in return. There is no selling involved, therefore no question of simony. The summoner became angry when I told him that his summonses had no validity in this priory and he started shouting at me. I thought he might become violent, so two of our brothers calmed him and showed him off our grounds.'

'The summoner is dead,' Richard said bluntly. 'As is Jane Henshaw, the girl who had the vision and became known as Jane the Healer.'

The prior made the sign of the cross. 'I am sorry to hear that.'

'I will be holding an inquest tomorrow at the eleventh hour, in the Court House.' Richard looked the prior straight in the eye. 'I would like you to attend.' *Will he dare suggest that the priory is not subject to the law of the land, I wonder?*

Prior Stephen bowed. 'But of course, Sir Richard. I will be there.'

As he turned onto the North Baileygate, the road that circled the base of the castle, Richard saw Doctor Jessop riding a pony towards him.

They both reined in, stopped and bowed to each other.

'Sir Richard, I must have words with you. I am most upset that you dared to remove Sir Nigel from my care. He may die as a result.'

'He was dying, Doctor Jessop. Taking his blood did not appear to be helping, and he deteriorated after you left.'

The doctor's cheeks grew red with anger. 'He needs to have blood removed. His liver is producing too much and it is clotting inside him to cause his paralysis. He should be moved to St Nicholas's Hospital at once, where I can treat him and remove the malevolent humour, and the monks there can look after him.'

Richard shook his head. 'It is poison that he is suffering from, not a humoral excess.'

'Poison! Poppycock! You dare question my medical skill? I am a physician and have studied at Oxford and St Bartholomew's Hospital in London.'

'I have no doubt —' Richard began, but was cut off by a shout from further down the road behind him.

'My lord,' called Hubert, riding up the road. 'You must come.'

Richard turned his horse around to meet him. 'What has happened?'

'The pilgrim, Timothy of Halifax, is dead. Lady Elizabeth de Ilkley discovered the body.' He glanced at Doctor Jessop then added, warily, 'It is not unlike the other one, the first we saw, my lord.'

'Show me,' returned Richard.

'A death?' queried the physician. 'Perhaps I should come too. And then we can continue our most important discussion.'

Richard nodded and they rode the short distance to Sir Baldwin de Ilkley's mansion. They dismounted and followed

Hubert around the mansion to find Sir Baldwin comforting his wife.

'About time, Sir Richard. This poor wretch crawled into our garden to kill himself in the middle of the night, I would say. We need to get him taken away before the folk of Pontefract start jabbering about the curse again. My little wife here won't go into the house until he is removed.'

'The poor man,' Lady Elizabeth muttered. 'Why would he do something like that? And why ... why in our garden?'

'We will deal with this as swiftly as possible, Lady Elizabeth,' said Richard. He bent to look closely at the gruesome sight. The hands were over the face, steepled to partially cover it, but with a thumb thrust into each eye. Jelly matter amid the congealed blood showed that both eyeballs had been punctured and their contents squirted out.

Touching the pilgrim's arms, Richard found they were cold and stiff. 'He has been here several hours, I believe,' he said as he felt in the dead man's habit for any personal possessions. He tapped the purse tied to the rope about his waist. 'He has not been robbed.'

A wooden staff lay close by, and beside it the silver pilgrim's badge that he had been robbed of in Wakefield when they'd first seen him. It had been twisted and bent out of shape.

Richard picked it up and hefted it pensively in his hand. 'It appears that before his death he tried to destroy this badge, which he said was his most precious possession.'

'You know him?' Sir Baldwin asked.

'He attended the Manor Court in Wakefield before I came here to Pontefract.'

'He was clearly mad,' said Doctor Jessop. 'The signs are all too clear. A violent self-murder. Look at the colour of his blood; it couldn't be blacker and has most foully clotted. This is because of excess black bile humour. It causes extreme melancholy, and when in this overabundance it produces madness.'

Richard straightened. 'I thank you for your learned opinion, Doctor Jessop.'

The physician nodded haughtily. 'Then you concede that I am the expert in physic. In that case, you will have my patient returned to me?'

'I will consider it, Doctor, but now perhaps you will take Lady Elizabeth inside her home and see if she would benefit from some of your physic. This has been a shock that no lady should have to see.'

Sir Baldwin put his arm about his wife's shoulder. 'This is a good idea, Elizabeth. Let us retire to the house with Doctor Jessop.'

Lady Elizabeth shivered and addressed Richard. 'And you will have the poor man's body removed?'

Richard bowed. 'I shall see to it directly.'

As they went down the garden path, he turned to Hubert. 'Ride for the castle and bring another coffin on the wagon. We will have another look at him in castle cell.'

An hour later, by the light of a lantern, Richard and Hubert looked at the body. With some difficulty, for the muscles had grown stiff, Richard removed the thumbs from the eye sockets with a sickening, sucking sound.

'Was the physician right, my lord? Was it an excess of black bile? Or could it be another effect of a curse? That's what the fellow was shouting out, as I told you. He wasn't happy about the sins he was seeing.'

'You also said that he had seen someone. Who was that?'

'I don't know, my lord. I left him at that point and went straight to meet you.'

Richard clicked his tongue. 'A pity. I have no doubt that Timothy of Halifax was murdered, just as Jane Henshaw and Simon of Holderness were slain and their deaths made to look otherwise. In the case of Jane Henshaw, it was made to look like self-murder because she had a vision. Simon of Holderness was silenced and murdered to look as if he had apoplexy. Doctor Jessop's assessment was nonsense. It was not Timothy's humours that were out of balance, but something he had seen.'

'You said that Jane Henshaw had been poisoned, sir. Could Timothy of Halifax also have been poisoned?'

'I think not. He had drunk much wine, but it was the fact that he was wandering about the town shouting about what and who he had seen that must have caused his death. He was silenced.'

'So he had seen the murderer?'

'Possibly. Or he had seen someone else and had to be silenced.'

'And why in Sir Baldwin de Ilkley's garden?'

'I think because it was close to the priory, where he was going. Or perhaps he was trying to go to All Saints' Church, on the other side of the Southgate. He may have been murdered not long after you saw him yesterday.'

Hubert punched one fist into the palm of his other hand. 'So now we have three murders.'

'No, Hubert. We have four. His Majesty was correct. Perkin Cratwell the executioner was also murdered.'

Hubert stared at him in surprise. 'But how do you know this, my lord? We have not seen his body. He was buried before we came to Pontefract.' He gave Richard a worried look. 'We are not going to have to dig him up, are we?'

'I haven't decided yet. But at the moment it is sufficient to know that he was murdered and probably by the same person, or persons, that killed these others.'

'But how do you know about Perkin Cratwell, my lord?'

Richard told him about the executioner's collections of trophy objects and of the ropes he had used. 'They all had a distinct noose. I presume it was one way that he had been shown when he began or which he later devised himself. Each noose was fashioned as a slipping knot, so that it could be passed over the head and then tightened about the neck. Each one had exactly eight coils holding the loop. However, on the rope that he had apparently used to hang himself, which Sir Nigel Fairfax had in his possession, there were only two crude coils. It had not been done by the same skilled hand. It smelled of dung, and when I visited the Stump Cross where he was found, there was dung on the crossarm of the cross. I am certain that he would have been killed in Pontefract and then taken at night to the Stump Cross in a gong wagon, hence the foul smell. There was nothing there for him to climb up on, so I think he was hauled up, probably by two men.'

'There are mysteries here and evil at work in Pontefract, my lord.'

'Indeed there are. I mean to try to flush the murderer out at the inquest tomorrow. So we will exhibit the bodies one by one. You will need the wagon and two men to take all three coffins to the Court House tomorrow, but before you do there will be work that I need you to do. But before I tell you, there is another task for you in the morning. I want you to find the gong farmer and also Sir Nigel Fairfax's cook. I think the best way of doing that is by asking around tonight and loosening a few tongues in the taverns of Pontefract.'

Hubert gave a wry grin. 'It will be a rare pleasure, my lord.'

Hubert knocked on Richard's chamber door an hour before the inquest was due to start. 'There was no sign of the cook, my lord. People knew him about the town, but he seems to have disappeared. I found the gong farmer, though.'

'Is he alive or dead?'

Hubert shook his head. 'Dead, I am afraid, my lord. His name was Freskin of Castleford. He lived a solitary life three miles outside the town, not surprising when you think of his work, shovelling the night soil and spreading it over fields. He would have been a stinky fellow. He was also a charcoal burner, and I was told where he lived. That's where I found him, his face and head all charred to a crisp in his own charcoal pile deep in the clearing where he lived in Barnsdale Wood.'

'What have you done with the body, Hubert?'

'I put it in his hovel of a house, to protect it from wild animals. I thought it best to see what you wanted me to do with it first.'

'Was there any sign of violence?'

'He was too charred to tell, but there was an empty flagon on the ground and a mug in his hand.'

'So now we have five murders, but almost certainly there have been others.'

'Shall I take you to see the body, my lord?'

Richard shook his head. 'There is not time, so we will have it collected later. We have the inquest to convene. So you need to do the work I told you about. I will see you at the Court House.'

The headborough's proclamation together with much cajoling by all of the guildmasters had worked, and the Court House was filled to capacity. Richard, wearing his judge's coif, was seated at the high bench above the three-sided box where witnesses had to stand. Sitting on one side were the jury of twelve men who had been selected to hear the cases. Opposite them at a small table was Basil of Darrington, ready with his parchments and writing paraphernalia. The local dignitaries and those who had come first were seated facing Richard, and behind them people were standing all the way to the great doors.

Richard started proceedings by rapping his gavel on a wooden block. As the hall fell silent, he introduced himself as the Circuit Judge for the King's Northern Realm, but also on this occasion standing in for Sir Nigel Fairfax to conduct the coroner's inquests. He nodded to Basil of Darrington to call out the first case.

'We begin with the case of Jane Henshaw, known as Jane the Healer. She was found dead two days ago in a chamber at St Mary Magdalene's Hospital, where she had been taken after falling ill.'

'Bring in the body,' Richard called out, picking up and ringing a bell at his side. Almost immediately, the court doors opened.

The audience had not expected this and there were gasps and mutters as Hubert came in, ahead of two soldiers carrying the coffin. They placed it on the floor in front of Richard's dais.

'Remove the lid,' Richard ordered.

Hubert did as bidden, then led the two soldiers from the court.

The crowd's reaction varied immensely. Some recoiled in revulsion, while others craned to see into the coffin. Wilfred Henshaw, Jane's father, covered his face and did not look.

'We have covered Jane Henshaw's body in a shroud, for she died from penetrating injuries with a bodkin in each eye. It may be that this happened during a convulsion.'

Richard then called several people to testify about the girdler's daughter and the remarkable things that had happened to her, and her untimely and sad death. First he called her father, who was so overcome with emotion that he could barely speak. Then he called and questioned Mother Cecilia, and lastly Sister Esmeralda.

To the last, he asked, 'From what you saw of her in the hospital, what conclusion did you come to?'

Sister Esmeralda was hesitant, but when she saw Richard's nod of encouragement, she stated, 'I think that she had probably been poisoned, my lord.'

'You are a simpler of physic and have experience of poisons that are used in small doses in physic?'

'I am, my lord.'

'In your opinion, what poison could have caused the state you found her in?'

'Two poisons, I believe. One is called orpiment, a yellow pigment that comes from a volcano, a mountain that spits out fire and molten rocks. When it is roasted, it becomes highly poisonous and can be made to disappear in water.'

'And what does it do to a person?'

'It makes them vomit and it gives a flux of the bowels. They become drowsy, speak and hear odd things and then they have fits.'

'And you think she could have had another poison?'

Sister Esmeralda nodded. 'By her fever, her red rash and flushing, and her difficulty breathing, I think she had the poison from belladonna — the deadly nightshade. It is a berry that can be found easily if one knows where to look. The two in combination would certainly have caused her fits.'

'No!' Wilfred Henshaw suddenly cried. 'Who would do such a thing to my beautiful daughter?'

Richard rapped his gavel and spoke sympathetically to the girdler. 'Master Henshaw, this is distressing to you, I know, but we are here to determine truths. This is important, for it will determine where your daughter is to be laid to rest.'

The girdler covered his face with his hands, leaned over his knees and wept.

Richard went on questioning Sister Esmeralda, and she told him of the friar who had come to sit and pray with Jane and of how he had said he had calmed her to sleep. Richard then announced that this friar had vanished.

'Would you wish me to ask the jury to rise while you address them, my lord?' Basil of Darrington asked.

'No, I am going to move to the second case straight away. I will instruct the jury when I am ready.' He rang the bell, and Hubert and the two soldiers brought in a second coffin.

As they laid it next to Jane Henshaw's, Hubert removed the lid to reveal a shrouded corpse. When they had left, Richard nodded to Basil of Darrington, who stood and announced the case.

'This is the case of Simon of Holderness, a Summoner to the York Consistory Court. He was found dead in his bed at the Pikestaff Inn the morning after Jane Henshaw's death.'

Richard then called for various witnesses, beginning with Harald Barrowman, then Bardolph and lastly Gertrude the bawd. They responded to Richard's questioning, all building up a picture of the summoner's dissolute and dishonest ways. Richard then called the three men whose names had been crossed off Simon of Holderness's list of people to summons. Without going into their actual misdemeanours, he asked them if they had been subjected to extortion by the summoner. All acknowledged that they had.

Richard then picked up the parchment that he had removed from the throat of the summoner and told the court of his findings of the rope marks on Simon's wrists and the use of a gag.

This provoked astonishment, anger and much noise that took several raps of Richard's gavel to quieten down.

'So, members of the jury, mark two other points here from these two cases. First a friar visited Jane Henshaw, yet we can find no trace of him. He did not belong to any of the religious orders in Pontefract. Note also from Harald Barrowman's testimony that the one-legged pilgrim has disappeared. We will now move straight to the third case.' He rang the bell again. 'Bring in the next body.'

For the third time, Hubert and the two soldiers brought in a coffin, placed it on the floor and removed the lid to reveal a shrouded body. At a gesture from Richard, Hubert and the two soldiers went and stood at the side of his desk.

Then Basil of Darrington announced, 'This third case is Timothy of Halifax, a wool merchant on pilgrimage to the tomb of Thomas of Lancaster in St John's Priory. His body was found in the garden of Sir Baldwin de Ilkley, which is not far from the priory.'

Richard called for testimonies from Lady Elizabeth, Sir Baldwin and then from Hubert.

'When you saw Timothy of Halifax in Pontefract, he was on his way to the priory; you say that he was drunk and shouting.'

'He was, my lord. He was shouting out about being cursed and seeing too many sins everywhere. And he cried that he had seen someone that should not have been there.'

Next, Richard had Prior Stephen take the stand and give his testimony. He replied to Richard's questioning, informing the court that Timothy had been drunk and was shouting angrily about being cursed. Two of his monks had had to encourage him to leave the priory.

'And so, members of the jury, I remind you all that the purpose of this inquest is to determine causes of death in these three cases. We have brought their bodies not to shock, which is why all three covered in shrouds, because sight of them would probably upset many. Yet they are here for a purpose. From what we have seen and heard, what say you about the cause of the death of Jane Henshaw? Confer and then the foreman of the jury will announce your opinion.'

It took but a few moments of exchanges before the foreman stood and announced, 'Murder!'

'And what of the case of Simon of Holderness?'

Again, the result was almost instant: 'Murder!'

'And of Timothy of Halifax?'

Once more, the conferring was short and the foreman's announcement emphatic: 'Murder!'

The angry calls from the crowd increased again, this time with people shouting out.

'The curses!'

'Sorcery!'

'Witchcraft!'

'No one is safe!'

'We'll all be murdered!'

Again, Richard's gavel gradually restored order. Finally, he nodded. 'Three murders, and they are all going to be investigated. The murderer or murderers, if there are more than one, shall be found and dealt with.'

He signalled for Hubert and the two soldiers to move forward to the coffins. To the audience's amazement, they lifted them one by one and propped all three against the high desk.

'Here is the reason I had the bodies brought in. I have one further question, but this time it is for the bodies of these unfortunate three people.' He waited, watching the whole courtroom carefully, then: 'Is anyone involved in your death nearby?'

The court buzzed with noise, then here and there someone shrieked. Soon they were all gesticulating and shouting in horror at the three coffins. All three bodies had started to seep bright red blood from the heads, soaking the shrouds.

'My lord, they bleed!' exclaimed Hubert.

'This is the sign of cruentation,' Richard called out. 'A murdered body will bleed in the presence of the murderer.'

Panic seized the crowd as people stared at each other, then at the bleeding bodies in their coffins. Richard surveyed the crowd to see if anyone gave themselves away. But again cries about curses, sorcery and witchcraft circulated about the large Court House.

'These three shall have justice. The law of the land will see that they are avenged and the evil killer or killers are punished. This inquest is now dismissed.'

CHAPTER ELEVEN

While Hubert and the soldiers took the coffins back to the castle in the wagon, Richard rode alongside the cart taking Mother Cecilia and Sister Esmeralda back to the hospital.

'I fear that those signs of murder will have an adverse effect upon the people of Pontefract, Sir Richard,' said Mother Cecilia.

Richard nodded. 'I am sure they will. It will certainly let the murderer know that I am determined to unmask him and bring him to justice.'

'But I think it may also unleash panic among the people of Pontefract,' she replied. 'Such a sign is a clear demonstration of the survival of the spirit after death. It will make people even more convinced that they died as the result of a curse, whether or not the actual tool of death was held by a human hand.'

Sister Esmeralda nodded in agreement. 'There were so many people shouting about the curses.'

Richard bit his lip meditatively. *Then perhaps I was wrong to get Hubert to position those flasks of pigs' blood in each coffin, so that when they were propped up they slowly trickled blood onto the shrouds. I had hoped to frighten the murderer sufficiently and cause him to reveal himself to me.*

Sir Nigel was actually sitting up in bed when Sister Esmeralda took over from the nun who had been left to watch him while she had attended the inquest.

'I feel as if I have been snatched back from the jaws of death,' he told them as Sister Esmeralda helped him to drink water. 'I just feel so weak.'

Richard asked Sister Esmeralda to give them a few moments alone so that they could discuss the inquest. The coroner listened with amazement as Richard told him the background to his visit to Pontefract, having been sent by King Edward of Caernarvon and Hugh le Despenser, and their belief that sorcery was being used in a plot to murder them.

'I had heard of this John of Nottingham case that is to be heard in the High Court,' Sir Nigel said. 'And I knew of the curse by Andrew Harclay upon the scaffold. I can see why people are talking of the two curses and sorcery.'

He listened further as Richard told him in detail about all three deaths and the results of the inquest. 'I may have made an error in using this subterfuge with the pigs' blood to simulate cruentation,' Richard conceded.

The coroner shrugged. 'Sometimes the law does need a helping hand. But there is little doubt that three murders have taken place.'

'There are at least two more, Sir Nigel. Perkin Cratwell was murdered and the act made to look like self-murder.' Richard described his examination of the rope collection and comparison with the rope used to hang the executioner, then his conclusion that Perkin's body had been taken to the Stump Cross in a gong wagon.

'Why, then, we need to find the gong farmer.'

'We have, and his body was found badly burned in his charcoal pit.' Richard leaned closer. 'And it is fortunate that Sister Esmeralda is so skilled that you are not the sixth murder that we know about. It is her belief that nightshade was used to poison you. It causes all of the symptoms that you exhibited, and had it been allowed to work fully, you would have stopped breathing. Your cook has gone missing, and I am sure he poisoned you. The reason, I think, was to prevent any coroner's investigations taking place. The murderer planned more deaths, like that of Freskin the gong farmer. Your cook had probably been an accomplice, but was expendable after Perkin Cratwell had been dispatched.'

Sir Nigel made the sign of the cross. 'I owe Sister Esmeralda my life. And you, Sir Richard, for she told me that you stopped Doctor Jessop from continuing to bleed me, which would only have made the poison more likely to do its worst.'

'But you are alive, and I must work hard to catch this murderer, for I fear there is more evil planned. There is something deep here, Sir Nigel, that I just cannot quite place my finger upon.'

'I will help you when I am back on my feet, Sir Richard. But with respect to the nuns and to Sister Esmeralda, I would feel better in my own bed.'

Richard smiled as he looked at the austere walls. 'I understand, and I will arrange for you to be taken home — and for Doctor Jessop to be barred from your home — and I will ask Mother Cecilia to allow Sister Esmeralda to continue to look after you. She is such a skilled healer.'

When Richard returned towards the castle, it was all too clear that the people of town were agitated. He dismounted and walked his horse so that he could overhear conversations as he passed. It seemed that it was just as Sister Esmeralda and Mother Cecilia had said; the cruentation that he had staged had made people imagine that they had witnessed God's verdict.

On reaching the castle he was immediately met by Martin of Helmsley, who bowed as the ostler took Richard's horse. 'Your pardon, Sir Richard. I am bidden by Sir Clifford to greet you as soon as you arrive and take you to the Great Hall.'

'The constable is feeling better, I take it?' Richard replied, removing his riding gauntlets.

'He is, Sir Richard. Yet he has guests that are most anxious to meet you.'

'Oh, who is so important that they want so urgent a meeting?'

'It is His Grace the Archbishop of York, Sir Richard, accompanied by Dean Walter Lydford, the Commissary General of the York Consistory Court.'

Archbishop William Melton was a fifty-year-old man with a dry, humourless face. Dressed in his white alb with a purple cincture about his waist and a violet zucchetto skullcap, he was sitting on one side of the fire in the Great Hall sipping wine from a silver goblet. Sir Clifford was on the other side of the fire, his bound leg outstretched before him. Another cleric, dressed in a long black gown adorned only with the plain silver crucifix hanging from his neck, was sitting beside the archbishop and in a corner, a smaller fellow dressed in a plain brown gown sat on a small stool with a pile of parchment scrolls beside him.

Martin of Helmsley announced Richard as he strode forward.

Sir Clifford attempted to stand with the aid of a stick, but was gestured to remain seated by Archbishop Melton, who stood and held out his hand.

'Sir Richard, this is His Grace William Melton the Archbishop of York. He honours us with this visit.'

Richard swallowed his pride and stepped forward as he was expected to do and kissed the cleric's hand. 'Your Grace,' he said.

'This is Dean Walter Lydford, my Commissary General. And his clerk Bartholomew Ditch.'

Richard bowed to Walter Lydford, whom he had heard of and knew to be referred to as Father Raven, and then acknowledged the clerk with a slight nod.

'I will come straight to the point, Sir Richard,' said the archbishop, sitting and placing his goblet on the floor beside him. 'I hear that you have held an inquest into the death of my summoner, Simon of Holderness.'

'Who was a most able apparitor,' added Walter Lydford. 'I have known him and used him for many years.'

'Then you may be disappointed to hear that we have evidence that he had been guilty of many sins himself. He used his position as a summoner to extort money from people and to pressure them into doing things. And yet, there is no doubt that he was murdered.' Richard quickly outlined the inquest findings on him.

'Also, you held an inquest on the girl, Jane Henshaw, who claimed to have had a vision of Thomas of Lancaster,' the archbishop persisted, without comment on the fact that the summoner had been murdered. 'This was not your concern, Sir Richard. This was a matter for the Consistory Court. The Commissary General of the York Consistory Court had already issued a summons for her to appear before him accused of blasphemy and charlatanry.'

'That summons was never served. She had died before the summoner, Simon of Holderness, could serve it. She, too, was murdered.' And again Richard gave them an outline of the inquest upon her.

'And you held an inquest on a pilgrim,' the archbishop stated, coldly. 'I question whether he could be called a pilgrim, since the Earl of Lancaster has never been canonised.'

'This pilgrim would have been brought before the court for idolatry,' said Walter Lydford.

Richard shook his head. 'Then that means that all of the pilgrims to the tomb of Thomas of Lancaster should be summoned to the Church Court. I fear you would never manage to see them all.' He raised his hands dismissively. 'But he, too, was murdered. That means all three deaths needed to be investigated by the Coroner's Court, which is what has happened. I acted on Sir Nigel Fairfax's behalf.'

In the distance outside, they could hear clamouring and shouting. Sir Clifford pointed to a window of the Great Hall. 'Do you hear that? The people of Pontefract have been stirred since the inquest you held. I am told by my servants that the town is being divided into two types of people. Those who are claiming Lancaster was a saint and others that he was a devil — that the so-called miracles he performed have brought nothing but unhappiness and tragedy.'

The archbishop picked up his goblet again. 'Tomorrow I shall go to the Monk's Hill where the Earl of Lancaster was executed as a traitor and I shall perform a cleansing ceremony. There shall be no more of this idolatry and blasphemy.' He sipped his wine and then dabbed his lips with the back of his hand. 'And then I shall pay a visit to St John's Priory and meet the prior. I shall demand that the gates be closed to the public and the tomb shall be cleansed.'

Richard shrugged his shoulders. 'That is entirely up to you, Your Grace. Although I understood that Prior Stephen does not accept your authority, which is in part why the gates were not closed already.'

Sir Clifford sat forward, looking very awkward. 'His Grace and I have already discussed this, Sir Richard. He knows of the mob that attacked myself and killed two of my men. I explained that I and Prior Stephen judged that it was best not to close the gates, lest we have even greater public disorder.'

Archbishop Melton ran a finger round the rim of the goblet. 'All this I accept. Yet we must suppress the idea that miracles are happening here. His Majesty is naturally upset about it, as his cousin was executed as a traitor to him. I have decided that the best course is to close the priory to the public and declare that these are not miracles, but merely wishful fantasies that have occurred. Then, when it is over, I shall hold healing services in the churches of All Saints and St Giles.'

Sir Clifford nodded enthusiastically. 'And order and normality will be restored.'

There was a loud hammering on the door, and Martin of Helmsley opened it and announced, 'Master Rupert Shenley, the Headborough of Pontefract.'

'Come, come, Master Shenley,' said Sir Clifford. 'His Grace the Archbishop of York has important work for you. At daybreak, you must issue a proclamation to tell the townspeople that a ceremony is taking place at the Monk's Hill and then at St John's Priory.'

The archbishop snapped his fingers and Bartholomew Ditch shot up from his stool and picked up the scrolls he had already prepared. 'Here is the proclamation; just make sure that all know of it, for we have an important spiritual task ahead to cleanse Pontefract of wickedness.'

This is definitely not the time to talk about the murder of Perkin Cratwell or of the gong farmer, Freskin of Castleford, Richard decided. *And yet it is curious that the archbishop seems blinkered and does not care much that people have been murdered, including his own summoner. He is more concerned about these supposed miracles than the murders.* He bowed. 'With your permission, I must leave.' He nodded to Rupert Shenley. 'Master Shenley is most effective with his proclamations, as I know from the attendance at the inquest today. So, I will leave these spiritual matters to Your Grace. Meanwhile, I will confine my attention to finding a murderer.'

'I think that our ploy may not have had the effect I had hoped for,' Richard said to Hubert that evening as they talked over the day's events in Richard's chamber over mugs of ale. On the table in front of him, Richard had been going over some of the parchments and palimpsests from the summoner's satchel.

'Why do you think there have been so many murders, my lord?'

'That is what troubles me, Hubert. We know that foul murders have been done and we have exposed them as such to the people of Pontefract, but we are no closer to knowing what links them. Yet it is indeed tempting to think that the curses are involved.'

Hubert stopped with his mug halfway to his mouth. 'What, do you mean that there might be something in these curses after all, my lord?'

'Not in any supernatural way, but I think they have something to do with them, yet what it is evades me.' Richard pushed the palimpsests to the side, then with a pensive frown he folded the one with what he thought was Latin doggerel and put it in his purse.

'So what must we do, my lord?'

Richard yawned. 'I think that I must sleep on it. Perhaps my dreams may help.'

After Hubert left, Richard made his ablutions and disrobed to prepare for bed. As he removed his shirt, he touched the chain of the St Christopher medallion that Lady Alecia and Wilhelmina had given him, and then as he removed his breeches he smiled at the garter that his fiancée had given him in their last private embrace.

He was still smiling when he got into bed. No dreams of solutions presented themselves to him that night, only images of Wilhelmina.

Four people met after the curfew hour, and once again the older man worked by the light of three black candles, making incantations over two waxen images.

'It has worked out as we planned,' said one.

'Except that dog of a lawyer has found out that murder was done,' snapped another.

'The bleeding corpses told the people that their murderer was present.'

'Pah! The dog played a trick on them, no more than that. We must all stay calm and remember our purpose.'

The older man continued his incantation as he heated the jaws of a pair of small tongs that he held by a cloth in the flame of a candle.

They watched as he applied the tongs to the neck of the first wax effigy. The wax immediately began to melt until the head hung at an unnatural angle. Then he did the same to the one next to it, until its head almost fell off.

All four began to laugh at the sight of the effigy, unmistakable with its small Archbishop's alb and mitre.

CHAPTER TWELVE

At the tenth hour the next day, the archbishop's party accompanied by a troop of the constable's soldiers — but without Sir Clifford himself, for he had not yet taken back to the saddle — ascended the Monk's Hill, where a huge number of people had already gathered. It was not a quiet assembly, for it seemed to hum like a swarm of bees, individual utterings being absorbed into a general angry buzz.

Rupert Shenley the headborough along with all of the local guildmasters was there, but without his wife. Similarly, Sir Baldwin de Ilkley and several other knights and yeomen and their servants were waiting on the far side of the great cross that had been erected where Thomas of Lancaster had been executed.

Richard and Hubert had followed the archbishop's party to lend legality to the proceedings. They sat upon their mounts and watched.

Archbishop Melton dismounted, as did all his party, including Walter Lydford and his clerk Bartholomew Ditch. The crowd parted as the archbishop approached the cross.

It was then that the noise of the gathering increased as people started talking louder and louder. Then they started to jostle back and forth in little pockets as it became obvious that this was not a unified meeting of people, but a crowd with different opinions, yet all mixed together rather than naturally separating into two factions.

And yet further on, apart from the crowd, making their way towards St John's Priory, where pilgrims were already clustered, was a group of slow-moving people from the Lazar House.

Then assorted cries rang out.

'Blessed Thomas!'

'Pah! Devil take him and his curse!'

'Give us more miracles!'

'No more deaths!'

'Tear down that cross!'

'Burn it!'

'Death to all sorcerers and witches!'

Hubert leaned towards Richard. 'I do not like this, my lord. It has the makings of a riot.'

As they looked around the crowd, they saw that some people were more vociferous than others. They saw Wilfred Henshaw shaking a fist at the cross.

'That curse killed my daughter!'

All around him supporters started shouting, but were immediately drowned by others proclaiming devotion to the blessed Thomas.

The archbishop raised his crosier, his staff shaped like a shepherd's crook, as if quieting a flock of sheep. 'My friends! Good people of Pontefract, look among yourselves. Can you not see the discord, the seeds of anger and unfriendliness that have been unleashed? We must calm them.'

'The curses!' an unidentified voice called out. 'We don't want them.'

'These lords curse each other and simple people get cursed, too,' cried another from a different part of the crowd.

Archbishop Melton raised his crosier for calm. 'My friends, you are correct; curses have no part in our belief. Only God alone can curse.'

'There are sorcerers and witches among us!' someone cried out.

Archbishop Melton nodded and raised his voice again. 'They are an abomination and what I do will help sweep them away. This is written in the Holy Book.'

He turned and held out his hand in Bartholomew Ditch's direction. The scribe immediately hurried forward with a large Bible held in both hands. Archbishop Melton then signalled for Walter Lydford to read from the book, translating the Latin into English with the ease of the scholar that he was.

'For this is written,' began the Dean of St Salvator's Church, 'in Deuteronomy, Chapter 18, verse 10. There shall not be found among you any one that maketh his son or his daughter to pass through the fire, or that useth divination, or an observer of times, or an enchanter, or a witch. Or a charmer, or a consulter with familiar spirits, or a wizard, or a necromancer. For all that do these things are an abomination unto the Lord, and because of these abominations the Lord thy God doth drive them out from before thee.'

Cries of 'Amen' went up around the crowd, and many spontaneously made the sign of the cross.

The archbishop again turned to Bartholomew Ditch and held out his hand. The clerk reached into his brown robe and drew out a cruet of water.

'Holy water,' cried the archbishop, raising it in the air. 'I am going to cleanse this area, this place where a man who had been declared a traitor to his anointed king was executed. This ceremony will take away the effect of any curse. It will become simple soil again.'

The crowd seemed to settle somewhat and was relatively quiet as the archbishop sprinkled water around the area, everyone falling back as he circled the cross, muttering a prayer and speaking in Latin all the time.

'We go now to the Priory of St John,' cried the archbishop when he had finished his cleansing ceremony.

Again the crowd parted as he, Walter Lydford and Bartholomew Ditch crossed the Monk's Hill and then walked the short distance towards the priory, where another crowd was waiting. As they did, Hubert pointed at several pilgrims who were scooping up the soil where the archbishop had scattered holy water.

'People will still worship here, I think, my lord,' he whispered.

'They will. But let us walk our horses and follow. Perhaps things will not be as smooth at the priory.'

The people in the crowd walking on either side of the archbishop, the dean and the clerk were not as emotionally quiescent as the archbishop would have liked. Some actively heckled him, others fawned over his words and still others pleaded with him not to disrupt the sanctity of Thomas of Lancaster's final place of repose.

'Surely you know that miracles have occurred here, Your Grace?' said a pilgrim. 'I am the living proof. I was lame but am now cured.'

'Blessed Thomas should be canonised, Your Eminence,' said another.

The archbishop smiled benignly at all, but refrained from getting into an argument or discussion as they walked. 'I will do what is best for Pontefract,' he announced.

Ahead of them near the priory gates, a man in a hood with his hands in his voluminous sleeves was checking that the dagger moved easily in the sheath he had strapped to his forearm.

A line of monks stood in front of the gates of St John's Priory. Prior Stephen of Cherobles was standing in the middle, his hands clasped in front of him. Behind them was a small crowd of people, including Father Percival and several of the more able-bodied people from the Lazar House.

'I told you this may not be so smooth,' Richard whispered to Hubert.

'Your Grace, you are welcome,' said Prior Stephen as the archbishop's party reached them, surrounded by the crowd.

'I thank you, Prior Stephen. I assume that you heard the proclamation, so you must know of my purpose.'

'It is not clear, Your Grace,' Prior Stephen returned.

'I am here to cleanse the execution ground and the tomb of Thomas of Lancaster, the cause of so much unhappiness and trouble.'

The prior frowned. 'We had some trouble some time ago when Sir Clifford de Mosley was injured and two men were sadly killed, but since the Priory Church has been freely open, there has been no trouble. We have only had miracles here.'

The archbishop snorted. 'You must have heard that there have been murders. There was an inquest yesterday, and the bodies of those poor murdered people bled in front of the whole town.'

So the archbishop did actually listen to me, Richard thought.

'I heard, Your Grace. Yet what proof is there that they are linked in any way to Thomas of Lancaster's tomb?'

'The curses!' cries went up.

'Sorcery and witchcraft.'

Prior Stephen shook his head. 'I dispute this, Your Grace.'

The archbishop pointed to the gates. 'I need to come in, Prior Stephen. I need to perform a cleansing ceremony.'

Prior Stephen shook his head again. 'I cannot permit this, Your Grace.'

Suddenly, Sir Baldwin de Ilkley and the other armed knights moved in front of the monks. 'And we, knights who were admirers of Thomas of Lancaster, will not permit his tomb to be desecrated or denigrated in any way. We will support the prior and his monks.'

All of his comrades raised gauntleted fists in support.

The officer in charge of the castle's soldiers leaned down towards the archbishop. 'Your orders, Your Grace?'

This provoked much jostling of the crowd. Some were for Sir Baldwin's intervention. Others, including Wilfred Henshaw and his supporters, were outraged by it.

'Now this I did not expect, Hubert,' Richard said. 'Sir Baldwin gives the impression of being staunchly against the idea of curses and of miracles, much as is Sir Clifford, yet here he is willing to prevent the Archbishop of York from carrying out a religious ceremony.'

'Should we intervene, my lord?'

'Not yet, Hubert. We just watch.'

Archbishop Melton raised his crosier and held up a hand. 'My friends, please. Let us always have peace.' Then to Prior Stephen: 'My purpose is merely to remove any possible malevolent forces with holy water and prayer. I and Walter Lydford need do no more than spend some time at the tomb on our own.'

'That I think I could permit, Your Grace, as long as you do nothing to desecrate the tomb.'

Sir Baldwin and his fellows and several of the monks protested to Prior Stephen, but he held up his hands. 'I,

Stephen of Cherobles, the prior of this holy church, welcome Archbishop Melton and Dean Lydford to enter our church to pray at the tomb of Thomas of Lancaster.'

Prior Stephen led the way through the gates towards the Priory Church. The crowds followed the archbishop and the dean and watched them enter and close the doors after them.

'Well, that went off more peacefully than it first seemed it would, my lord,' said Hubert.

'Indeed. If it does work and reduce the fears of the people of Pontefract about the curses, then that can only be a good thing. We shall then have no other distraction and can get on with finding the murderer of these poor folk.'

After some minutes, one of the doors opened and the archbishop stepped out from the shadows within. The figure of Walter Lydford stood immediately behind and to the side of him, with his hood pulled down.

'Good people of Pontefract,' called out the archbishop, raising his crosier and his other hand. 'We have contemplated the wrongs that have been done here in Pontefract. Of most importance, I hereby nullify and abolish the curse that Thomas of Lancaster, an acknowledged traitor to his anointed king, Edward of Caernarvon, made against Andrew Harclay, the Earl of Carlisle and against all of his followers.'

Hubert stared at Richard in astonishment. 'What is he saying?'

All around, people appeared dumbfounded. And then there were mixed reactions. Some cheered and laughed. Others shook their fists at the archbishop.

Prior Stephen stood shaking his head in disbelief.

'Furthermore,' called out the archbishop, 'we are now going to de-sanctify the tomb of Lancaster, the traitorous earl, and cleanse this priory, which shall be shut down.'

'No!' cried Prior Stephen.

'Never!' shouted Sir Baldwin as he and his men drew swords and ran towards the church.

'*In nomine Patris et Filii et Spiritus Sancti,*' said the archbishop, signing the cross before stepping back into the church. The doors slammed shut and the sound of bolts being rammed home rang out.

Sword pommels crashed against the great wooden doors and the crowd, now transformed into a mob, ran at the doors, some to lend fists, others to try to drag the knights away. Fights broke out, and people tried to get out of harm's way.

Richard and Hubert made their way through the crowd to pull Prior Stephen to safety.

'The archbishop has made matters a hundred times worse. Is there another way into the church?' Richard asked the prior.

'Yes, from the chapter house into the west transept. This way.'

They weaved their way through the crowd and went round the building to enter the chapter house, where a single monk was kneeling in prayer. He was clearly frightened by the noise of the mob outside.

'Has anyone come this way from the church?' Richard asked.

'No, sir. The door is bolted from here.'

Wasting no time, Hubert pulled back the heavy bolts and threw open the door. They all rushed into the transept then turned along the aisle towards the high alter.

There they found Walter Lydford lying face down on the floor in front of the tomb of Thomas of Lancaster. He was dressed only in his undergarments; his black robe had gone. Blood trickled down his neck from a nasty blow to the back of his head. There was no sign of the Archbishop of York, apart from his mitre and crosier, which were lying on the floor as if he had just vanished into thin air.

The banging on the doors was almost deafening, but still they stood firm.

'Thank the Lord,' said Richard, bending to examine the prostrate figure. 'The dean is merely knocked out.'

There were running footsteps behind them, and they all turned to see Bartholomew Ditch run in, still clutching the Bible and the archbishop's cruet.

'There!' Richard said, pointing to the Lazar window. 'That is where he went.'

'Look, my lord,' said Hubert, pointing to a pentagram figure daubed in blood on the honey stone of the tomb. 'The tomb has been desecrated.'

'That is the dean's blood, I will wager,' said Richard. 'But this is starting to make some sense.'

'My poor master,' moaned the clerk, bending over the still unconscious Dean.

'Master Ditch, were you aware of Simon of Holderness's notes he made of cases? Did he use Latin much?'

The clerk wore a pained expression. 'He knew only a few words, Sir Richard. But he had his own shortened method of writing that he mixed up with it.'

Richard quickly opened his purse and drew out the folded palimpsest, smoothing it on the tomb. 'Can you read these lines? I think I have worked some of them out.'

Bartholomew Ditch leaned over it, knitting his brows thoughtfully as Richard pointed to the lines:

ab m n ex swin
fac pec pon
pat ex nec alc

dom puel
ego peric

'I think the last two lines could be "*domum puellae*" and "*ego periculum*,"' said Richard. '"The girl's house" and "I am in danger."'

'Yes, I see,' said the clerk. 'Well, "*ab m*" was his way of writing Archbishop Melton; "*n*" would be "nun", and "*ex*" would be "excommunicated".'

'What about "*swin*"?'

'That would be "Swine Nunnery". It is a Cistercian nunnery near Holderness. So "*fac pec*" is his abbreviated Latin for "*facit peccatum*": "lives in sin."'

Richard snapped his fingers. 'And so "*pon*" refers to Pontefract.'

Prior Stephen was also leaning over now, puzzling over the palimpsest. 'I think "*pat*" would be "*pater*", meaning "father." Therefore, "*ex*" again stands for "excommunicated" and "*nec alc*" means "necromancy and alchemy."'

Bartholomew Ditch stood straight. 'Archbishop Melton had trouble with several nuns who were excommunicated. One was Joan of Leeds, and another was one who absconded from Swine Nunnery. She was a skilled simpler, if I recollect, and feigned her own death by taking a poison. She made a dummy of herself that was buried by others who colluded with her.'

Richard patted the clerk on the shoulder. 'Good work, Bartholomew Ditch. Now you and Prior Stephen look after the dean. Time is of the essence. Hubert and I must go to prevent further profanity and tragedy. Wipe away this blood from the tomb, wait some minutes and then open the doors. When the people see that the archbishop is not here and the tomb is not despoiled, they will calm down. The knights and the constable's men should help restore calm.'

Hubert did as Richard ordered him and after requisitioning the first horse he could, rode swiftly for town. He dismounted a street away from the address he was to go to and walked the rest of the way on foot.

'Whatever happens, make sure no harm comes to Sister Esmeralda,' Richard had said. 'When you come upon the house, keep your eyes about you, for the murderer may be going to the same place.'

Hubert strove to look nonchalant, rather than someone walking with a purpose. As he turned up a narrow street, he walked past a man with a liripipe hat pulled down low over his face. Yet as they passed, he was sure that he recognised the jaw, from his days in the army. An amusing fellow who could always tell a merry tale, could juggle spoons, mugs or even daggers. A fellow who never lost at Hazard, but who was always generous to his opponents. Except during battle. He was deadly with a bow, fierce with a sword and a veritable devil with a bollock dagger. Hubert remembered seeing how he'd used the latter at the Battle of Boroughbridge, after they had won. The images flashed before him in a moment, and he knew it was him. He spun round and grabbed the end of the liripipe to pull it back, revealing a tonsured head. At the same moment, the man also spun round, and Hubert just caught the glint of a dagger in his hand.

He felt an excruciating pain and tumbled towards the ground, clutching his chest.

Richard had further to ride, but just as he had told Hubert to do, he dismounted and made the rest of his way on foot.

I have been such a fool. I was trying to see the connections between the murders, when they were not directly linked. Yet each had a logic; they had to follow one another. And yet I fear that this devilish plan has still far to play out.

Richard mounted the wooden steps and slowly made his way up to the ledge with its wooden door.

I thought I recognised something. Indeed, I should have noticed the other.

He found the door easy to open, for it had no lock and no bolts. It was dark inside, and there was no one present in the rock-hewn chapel. Going silently with his hand upon the pommel of his sword, he found the small corridor that led down the steps of the beautifully carved spiral staircase leading to the living chamber and the well.

I dare not strike a light lest I alert the hermit, but I am like a mole in a hole down here.

He drew his sword and descended slowly. He reached the bottom step and placed a foot down, only to find it suddenly slipping on a number of small greasy balls of some sort. Unable to get his balance, he dropped his sword and tumbled forward, falling down the well, hitting water and then striking rock.

Like a rat … I … fell … into … his trap.

And then he knew nothing as his lungs started to suck in water.

CHAPTER THIRTEEN

Richard felt as if he was dreaming of drowning in a water-filled chasm. Then as he gagged, he immediately opened his eyes, but saw nothing. With alarm, he realised that he was actually upside down, underwater. He stopped himself from breathing and tried to spew out the water he had taken in. It was not easy, for it was pitch-dark and he was completely submerged.

But at last, he managed to turn over and break the surface into the darkness of the well. He coughed and spluttered.

At least I can put my feet on the bottom. But how far is the top of this well?

He tried to launch himself upwards, but without success, for the water dragged on him. The top seemed far out of reach. He felt around the walls of the well to see if he could find handholds or footholds, but it had been scraped or carved so well that he could gain no purchase. He tried to wedge himself against one wall and use his feet and elbows to move up it, spider-like. But that too failed, for he could not reach across to the opposite side.

The hermit may never come back and I may die here, he thought in a forlorn moment. *And I may never hold my Wilhelmina again. I may not —*

Then he snapped his fingers.

Wilhelmina, of course!

He reached under his shirt and pulled off the St Christopher medallion and chain that she and Lady Alecia had given him for protection. He unclasped it and pulling out his dagger, made a loop round the pommel.

Now if I can use it as a grappling hook, perhaps —?

He tossed it several times as high as he could, retaining the end in his hand. But each time it clanged against the well wall and fell with a splash.

Then in his mind he heard her, in that last moment they had shared at Sandal Castle in Wakefield, when she'd given him her garter so that they could feel as if they were together.

Quickly, he removed the garter and retied it on the end of the chain. Testing the whole thing, he was not sure if it would be long enough or strong enough. But it was his only chance.

In the dark he whirled it round and round and muttered a prayer before he tossed it upwards.

Archbishop William Melton did not know where he was or who had forced him at knifepoint to say the things he had at the door of the Priory Church. When he and Walter Lydford had entered the church, they had thought they would be alone, but two monks were waiting for them. At least, they had thought they were monks, until the dean was struck and knocked senseless, while a knife blade was put to his own throat and he was told precisely what to do and what to say by the one who had donned Lydford's robes and stood behind him with the blade in his back.

Then when the other bolted the doors, he had a gag tied about his mouth and his mitre was thrown aside and replaced by a sack so that he could see nothing. They pulled a monk's habit over him before he was rushed across to the Lazar window, where one went through and the other forced him to follow. All the time he knew that a false move would likely result in his swift death. He had heard the resultant clamour but could do nothing but walk between the two men, as if they were three of the Cluniac order. Once they emerged from the enclosed tunnel that had been built along the east wall of the church, they were soon absorbed in the milling throng and the two assailants were able to push their way out of the priory grounds and through the gates.

That was as much as he knew, because he could see nothing and do nothing except be guided and pushed by them. It was a difficult walk uphill, towards the castle, he imagined. Then downhill again before rising towards the town. He was taken at last into a building of some sort and made to sit down as he was tied up. The room was almost unbearably hot from a roaring fire. With the gag tied about his face and the sack over his head, he could not even ask what they intended to do to him, or why.

He heard hushed voices, one of them a woman's. Exactly how many voices, he could not be sure. He thought that the one who had wielded the knife had gone, for he heard a door open and close. Then the voices subsided, except for one, which seemed to keep up some garble in a language that he could not understand; he only knew that it was something repeated over and over.

How long it went on like that he did not know, until it abruptly stopped and the sack was pulled from his head.

Blinking in the firelight, he saw that there were three people in the room. A man holding the sack, a woman staring at him with obvious contempt in her eyes, and an old man dressed in a dusty robe with long, unkempt grey hair and a bushy, braided beard, who was sitting at a table muttering over half a dozen wax effigies, each the length of a man's arm.

As the old man turned to look at him, he saw how much he and the woman resembled one another.

'Welcome, Archbishop William Melton,' the old man said. 'It has been many years since you wronged me and excommunicated me. Do you remember me, you dog?'

The prelate slowly shook his head.

'Perhaps it would be easier if we removed the gag,' the old man said, gesturing to the man holding the sack.

'A single word out of place or an attempt to call out, and your life will be snuffed out by our friend. He has been itching to kill someone ever since his former master, the coroner Sir Nigel Fairfax, failed to die from the poison he had been so patiently feeding him.'

The gag was removed and in its place a crude noose was dropped over his head and pulled tight enough to make the archbishop realise how quickly he could be dispatched.

'I ... I heard about Sir Nigel,' he said.

The woman sneered. 'You didn't answer my father, Your Grace.'

The archbishop looked from the woman to the old man and back again. 'Sir Peter Fitzjohn? Is that you?'

'It is I,' the old man admitted. 'You and your infernal Church Court summonsed me for necromancy and alchemy. You excommunicated me six years ago, and that dog on the throne dispossessed and stripped me of my title and gave my lands to his cousin Thomas of Lancaster. That was when they were still friends, before Lancaster turned traitor. I came to Pontefract, where I knew of the cave that two previous hermits had worked on. I had visited them when visiting my lands nearby. And so, I became Peter the Hermit.' He suddenly laughed. 'It was hard work carving that cave, but it gave me time to perfect my studies in the occult arts, and no one bothered me. I had brought my occult tools with me and had no need of money, for the people of Pontefract wanted me to tell fortunes and give prophesies in return for food and drink.'

The door opened and Rupert Shenley the headborough came in. The archbishop gasped as he recognised him.

'So you have not yet done the deed?' Rupert asked, taking his place by the woman and reaching for her hand.

'And do you recognise me?' she asked the cleric. 'If you think of me wearing a nun's habit, perhaps that will refresh your memory. I also was excommunicated by you, because I left the nunnery for love.'

'Brenda of Swine!' the archbishop exclaimed. 'You absconded from the nunnery. You made the other nuns think you were dying of the smallpox. You made a dummy of yourself that was buried. We only found out when a sister was so overcome with guilt that she confessed to assisting you.'

'I was thirty-four when I was forced to go into that nunnery, when my father was dispossessed and excommunicated. It was a living hell from which I thought I would never escape — until I met my future husband.'

The headborough squeezed her hand. 'As a wool merchant I had visited the holy houses from Hull and Beverley in the east to Lancaster in the west. At Swine Nunnery, near Holderness, I met and fell in love with Brenda, who came with me to Pontefract and became Bernice.'

'And when my father heard about the headborough's new wife and I was described to him, he made contact again and we occasionally were able to meet as father and daughter when I visited Peter the Hermit in his hermitage.'

'I had no love for Edward the tyrant and still less for Lancaster, the usurper of my lands,' the hermit went on. 'When their petty squabbles became rebellion and Lancaster was beheaded, I was happy, especially when my own nephew, Andrew Harclay, was the person who had captured him and brought about his ignominy.'

The archbishop stared at him in astonishment. 'You were related to Andrew Harclay, the Earl of Carlisle?'

'He was my nephew, and his sister Lady Sarah Harclay is my niece. His mother Joan Fitzjohn was my sister.'

Bernice Shenley snorted. 'Then the so-called miracles started being reported and people began calling him St Thomas!'

'Worse,' added Rupert Shenley, 'because of his supposed saintliness, the curse he had made on Sir Andrew and the King and Hugh le Despenser was given credence.'

'And when Sir Andrew was declared a traitor by that idiot of a king, who ordered that my cousin should be butchered to death, we all decided that justice must be done.'

Peter the Hermit pointed at the wax effigies and held up two that represented King Edward and Hugh le Despenser. 'My brother in the occult arts, John of Nottingham, was commissioned by twenty-three burghers of Coventry to use necromancy to dispose of the King and his acolyte, Despenser. Unfortunately, he was denounced by the miserable assistant, Robert Marshall, and is at this time languishing in Coventry dungeon awaiting trial. But I have been using the same methods, harnessing the same forces to bring death to all who brought the name Harclay into such disrepute.'

He gave a cruel laugh and laid the wax dolls on the table and picked up two others. They both had clerical robes on. One had a nose like a raven and the other wore a mitre. 'Do you recognise yourself and the dean of your court? Notice how their heads and necks have been melted.'

'That... That is me?'

'It is,' returned the hermit, picking up a piece of cord that was looped around the neck of the archbishop's effigy. 'And it has brought you here to Pontefract, just as it was supposed to.'

'To face your end!' Bernice Shenley snapped, nodding at the cook, who suddenly raised the rope about the archbishop's neck, pulling his head up.

'But … why?' he managed to gasp.

'Because you excommunicated us. Now you have served your purpose. You nullified Lancaster's curse, so there is no more curse upon Andrew Harclay or the family. The news will soon spread about the country, and people will recognise Lancaster for the traitorous dog he was, not think of him as a saint. Now, Sir Andrew's curse is the only one that is active. The only one that people will talk about.'

'But … what will you do … now?'

'Simple,' Bernice replied. 'You are going to your death here and now, in our presence. Later, you will be found hanging from the cross upon the Monk's Hill. A confession of guilt will be on your body.'

'Then we will continue with our purpose and concentrate on killing the King,' added her father, Peter the Hermit. 'And the way that we did it, through necromancy and the occult arts, will be revealed as the new religion, the new power. Our lands will be restored to us, as will our power to choose our own king to take Edward the fool's place.'

Suddenly, the door was thrown open and Richard burst in. His arm rose and whipped forward to toss his dagger, which plunged into the cook's heart. This had barely registered with the others in the room when Richard launched himself at the headborough and punched him in the face, breaking his nose in a spray of blood and propelling him backwards to strike his head with a sickening thud against the wall. He slid down, unconscious.

Richard turned just in time to dodge Bernice, who went for his eyes with her fingers bent like claws. She still managed to rake a cheek, drawing three blood streaks across it, but he grabbed a wrist, twisted her arm behind her back and subdued her by throwing a monk's habit over her head and wrapping the waist cord about her so she could not move her arms.

Richard heard a gurgling noise and spun round to see the old hermit pulling the noose tight about the archbishop's neck, causing his eyes to bulge and his face to turn puce. Flipping the cook's body over with his foot, in one movement he pulled out the dagger from his chest and tossed it to skewer the old man's arm and cause him to stagger back against the wall.

'I heard all of your confession to the archbishop,' he said as he removed the garrotte from the prelate's neck. 'So now I want the whole truth about why you killed so many innocent people.'

Peter Fitzjohn gave a throaty laugh. 'Not one of them was innocent.'

'You ... you killed my summoner, Simon of Holderness,' said the archbishop as he rubbed his throat. 'Why?'

'We decided he had to die because he had seen me and my husband,' said Bernice Shenley. 'And he had also identified Gladwin, the instrument of our revenge, because he had shared the same harlot. Gladwin was only suspicious of that, until the summoner confessed when Gladwin had his hands upon his throat.'

'I had realised that he had seen one of you,' Richard said. 'He had made notes, which I was only able to decipher with the help of Bartholomew Ditch and the dean after you had kidnapped the archbishop. It became apparent that it was you, the excommunicated nun that he had seen, who was living in sin in Pontefract. Timothy of Halifax, the pilgrim, was killed because he had also seen you, hadn't he? He was in danger of making your secret public knowledge.'

Bernice sneered. 'As a wool merchant he knew my husband, and when he saw me with him in Pontefract he began to shout, for he too had seen me in Swine Nunnery. Gladwin followed him and decided he had to be silenced immediately.'

'But there had been no miracle. His sight had not actually been restored,' said Richard. 'I imagine it was not so bad as all that in the first place. He just wanted a miracle. I believe that is why he was killed in Sir Baldwin de Ilkley's garden. He had thought he was going to the Church of All Saints.'

The archbishop shook his head in disbelief. 'Wickedness! But why did the girl have to die? She was going to be summoned to the Ecclesiastical Court.'

'They poisoned her and then murdered her in cold blood to further discredit Thomas of Lancaster, Your Grace,' said Richard. 'It was to give credence to the idea that Andrew Harclay's curse could outmatch that of Thomas of Lancaster's.'

Peter Fitzjohn, the erstwhile Peter the Hermit, was clutching his arm, still with the dagger sticking through it, blood flowing from the wound. He began to laugh. 'And his curse was stronger. It has worked. We have brought unrest, fear and now wholesale disorder to Pontefract. And we shall still succeed in all of our endeavours. You cannot stop it. Gladwin is unstoppable, the most perfect killing instrument. He served loyally in Andrew's army, as did you, Sir Richard.'

Richard felt a slight pang of guilt as he always did when he thought of his old commander's grisly end. 'I did, and I was proud to serve under him.'

'Then join us!' said Bernice.

Richard shook his head. 'I disapprove of the murder of innocent people. And what you have been doing is utterly evil. Your instrument of death killed Perkin Cratwell, did he not? I did not understand why he was killed at first, because I was looking for a link, but there wasn't one, was there? It was pure revenge.'

'Of course it was,' said the hermit. 'He was the King's executioner. He executed Lancaster and he murdered my nephew by hanging, drawing and quartering him. He had to die, just as the friar at my nephew's execution had to die, and the messengers who carried his poor body parts to cities around the country. With each additional outrage, it was building up the list of crimes the King must answer for with his life.'

'And this creature of yours, this Gladwin, killed Freskin of Castleford, the gong farmer, in case he talked too much and made people aware that Perkin Cratwell had not committed self-murder. And yet you should now realise that His Majesty was not convinced that he had killed himself. He believed that it was death by sorcery, hence he sent me to investigate. And that was your undoing. I know all about this man, about the way he sneaks around the country adopting the guise of a friar to murder people such as Jane Henshaw, or dressed as a one-legged pilgrim to murder Simon the Summoner.'

Bernice Shenley smiled thinly. 'We are not undone, merely a little bruised. Soon our Gladwin will come to finish you, once he has removed Sir Nigel Fairfax and the nun, Sister Esmeralda. If it had not been for her, he would have been dead already.'

Archbishop Melton stared at her in horror. 'Have you no shame? After all of this evil you have done, you have sent an assassin to murder a coroner and a nun!'

She sneered. 'As I said, Gladwin will soon return and then he will kill you both.'

The door suddenly burst open, and she laughed triumphantly as a man flew into the room.

'Gladwin! Kill them —' she began.

But then she saw that the man was not rushing but was stumbling forward, his feet hobbled with a rope tied round them. He teetered for a few moments then fell on his front on the reed-covered floor, his face a mass of blood and bruises, all discoloured in stark contrast to the whiteness of his tonsured head. One arm seemed to have landed at an unnatural angle.

Hubert stepped into the room and stomped a boot on the man's back. 'Meet Gladwin Tuke, my lord,' he said. 'We had a disagreement in the street outside Sir Nigel Fairfax's house where you sent me. I recognised him, and he took offense when I pulled off the liripipe he was wearing and tried to stab me. Fortunately, as you know, I was wearing my crusader's arrow and nothing can harm me. His blade bounced off it and so I had to teach him some manners, then persuade him to tell me where I needed to take him. I am afraid I had to break an arm and pull a shoulder out of joint.'

The man Gladwin was barely conscious, but he groaned, almost at the same time as Rupert Shenley the headborough started to rouse. But clearly there was no fight left in either man.

'It is still too late, Sir Richard,' said the old man. 'You cannot reverse what we have done and what these wax effigies will still do. The King, Despenser, the archbishop and all those who have wronged us are doomed by the spells I have cast.'

Hubert looked in horror at the wax dolls. 'What devilment is this, my lord? Was His Majesty right after all? Were these murders by sorcery?'

Richard shook his head as he gathered up all of the wax figures. 'They are nothing, Hubert. They have no power and are of no importance.' He looked at the archbishop and held the effigies up. 'Do you agree, Your Grace?'

The prelate nodded his head emphatically. 'I think the less that is known about this the better. We must dispel the notion that sorcery can do anything. All of these murders that they have confessed to were done by human planning and involved human hands.'

Richard crossed to the fire. 'I totally agree, so let us simply get rid of them.' With which he cast them on the fire and they started to melt.

He turned to the old man. 'It is now as if they never existed. Yet you villainous four will face charges of multiple murder and will face justice.'

'Never!' cried the old man, pulling the dagger from his arm and immediately shoving it into his own throat. An arc of blood erupted from the severed arteries and he slowly slumped to the floor.

Bernice screamed and cried out piteously, 'Father!'

But no one in the room felt any pity whatsoever for her.

Archbishop Melton looked at them in disgust. 'You will all be excommunicated and therefore will go to your deaths without the benefit of a priest.'

'You will be tried in a court of law,' Richard said. 'His Majesty, King Edward will be informed of your treason and your cold-blooded murders. And you know what an unforgiving sovereign he is. I do not personally believe that Sir Andrew Harclay deserved his horrible death, but you all most certainly do.'

EPILOGUE

King Edward did not choose to be lenient. When the three remaining traitors were brought before the High Court, he demanded that they should face the full sentence as prescribed by the law.

A proclamation was made that Archbishop Melton had been kidnapped by a murderous group and had been forced at knifepoint to say the things he had. He performed a fresh cleansing ceremony at the tomb of Thomas of Lancaster to remove any of the malevolence that the traitor Gladwin and his accomplice, the cook, had defiled the church with. In addition, he and Dean Walter Lydford visited the hermitage and again performed a cleansing ceremony, to consecrate it for the use of any legitimate hermit in the future.

Inquests were held on the deaths of Perkin Cratwell and Freskin of Castleford, both of whom were deemed to have been murdered by the group. The executioner's body was exhumed and reburied in the cemetery at St Richard's Friary, but in light of the evidence that Freskin of Castleford was at least an accomplice to the hanging of Perkin Cratwell, he was posthumously excommunicated and was thence interred in the grave vacated by the executioner's body.

Richard stayed in Pontefract long enough to see Sir Clifford de Mosley and Sir Nigel Fairfax both recover to full health. He was not surprised to learn that Sir Nigel had fallen in love with Sister Esmeralda and had asked her to consider leaving her order to marry him. He felt sad for the coroner when she most politely declined, for she had taken a vow and considered herself to be already married to God.

As Richard and Hubert rode back to Wakefield, they talked of the whole Pontefract affair. Hubert again returned to the subject of his crusader's arrow and its incredible power.

'But, my lord, you told me that you fell into the well at that hermitage, but you did not tell me how you managed to climb out.'

'I used a charm that Lady Alecia and Lady Wilhelmina gave me. It was a St Christopher medallion. I tied it to my dagger and was able to use it like a grappling hook to pull myself up.'

He said nothing about Lady Wilhelmina's garter, without which he would probably have perished in the well. Unconsciously, his hand went down to touch his thigh and he smiled as he felt the garter through the material. Wilhelmina had saved him and thereby saved the archbishop, the King and the chamberlain. He vowed that the garter would always be with him.

'So now do you believe in charms and talismans, my lord?' Hubert asked with a grin. 'After all, we both have the proof that they work.'

Richard grinned back. 'You know, Hubert, I think I do.'

A NOTE TO THE READER

Dear Reader,

Thank you for taking the time to read my novel. *The Summoner's Sins* is a work of fiction, yet as with the novel before it, *The Pardoner's Crime*, the location, many of the main characters and certain events are historical facts around which the story was woven. The places within and around Pontefract, including the famous Pontefract Castle, the Hermitage, St John's Priory, St Richard's Friary, St Mary Magdalene's Hospital and the Lazar House were all real. Today, only the ruins of the castle and the hermitage, with its well, remain for people to see. The basic geography of the medieval town is still present as it is described in this novel.

Thomas, Earl of Lancaster was indeed executed outside Pontefract Castle on 22nd March 1322 after being defeated at the Battle of Boroughbridge on 16th March 1322, by Sir Andrew Harclay. Lancaster regarded his capture as the ultimate betrayal, since he had knighted Harclay in 1303. Accordingly, he cursed Harclay, King Edward and Hugh le Despenser and he prophesied that Harclay would die a traitor's death within a year. Three days after Lancaster's execution, King Edward II made Harclay the first Earl of Carlisle. The curse seemed to come true, however, for almost a year later Harclay was found guilty of treason and executed, as recounted in this novel, and suffered death by being hanged, drawn and quartered, without the benefit of a trial. His head was placed on a spike on London Bridge and his other quarters were nailed to the gates of Carlisle, Newcastle, Bristol and Dover. In 1328 his sister,

Sarah Harclay, was permitted to reclaim his body parts for a Christian burial.

Within days of Lancaster's execution, miracles were being reported, including some of those alluded to in this work. A cult quickly arose, much to the annoyance of the King and his chamberlain, Hugh le Despenser. King Edward did his best to suppress it and ordered the Constable of Pontefract Castle to close the gates of St John's Priory to prevent pilgrims worshiping at the tomb beside the high altar. The constable, Richard Moseley, was injured and two of his men, Richard Godeley and Robert de la Hawe were killed. The King also ordered the Archbishop of York, William Melton, to suppress the cult, which he duly tried to do.

Nevertheless, the cult actually gathered momentum. Indeed, after Edward II's deposition in 1327, the cult was no longer banned. His son, King Edward III and Archbishop Melton attempted to have Lancaster canonised, a first step towards becoming a saint. In that year, Edward III allowed the priory and convent of Pontefract to build a chapel on the Monk's Hill, where the Earl had been executed.

The power of the Church was immense in those days, and the Church Courts could hand out many punishments for moral misdemeanours, the ultimate being excommunication. It is recorded that Archbishop Melton had several dealings with nuns and monks who absconded from their orders, and excommunication was the result. A noted example of this was Joan of Leeds, mentioned in this book, who absconded from the nunnery of St Clement's by York in 1318, to go to Beverley to live in sin with a man. She had feigned a fatal illness and fashioned a dummy of herself, which her fellow nuns buried.

Sorcery, necromancy, curses and counter-curses were all things to fear in the medieval period. The central feature of this novel revolves around a plot to kill the King and his favourite, Hugh le Despenser. Once again, this is based on recorded facts. In November 1323 a necromancer, John of Nottingham, was commissioned by twenty-eight burghers of Coventry to use sorcery to kill King Edward, Hugh le Despenser, his father Hugh le Despenser Snr and the Prior of Coventry. They provided him with money, a remote manor house outside Coventry, seven pounds of wax and two yards of cloth, with which he fashioned effigies of them. In order to try out the sorcery, he used effigies of the prior's steward Nicolas Crump and other officials and an unpopular local man, Richard de Lowe. In May 1324, the necromancer and his assistant, Robert Marshall, performed a ritual killing on the effigy of Richard de Lowe by inserting a heated lead pin into the effigy's head. The following morning, the victim was found by his servants to be writhing in agony in his bed with headache. Some days later, John of Nottingham pulled out the lead pin and shoved it into the effigy's chest. The victim died soon after.

Robert Marshall was badly frightened by this and confessed to a local magistrate, whereupon all concerned were arrested and brought before the King's Bench later in the year, charged with the murder of Richard de Lowe. A jury found them innocent. John of Nottingham died mysteriously in prison.

So frightened was Hugh le Despenser by this attempt at murder by sorcery that he wrote to Pope John XXII asking for his protection against further attacks by magical means. The Pope replied that he should 'turn to God with his whole heart and make good confession,' which would be all the help he would need.

In 1326 Hugh le Despenser was executed with great brutality in Hereford. As for King Edward, he was forced to abdicate in favour of his son on 20th January 1327. He was reported to have died on 21st September 1327 in Berkeley Castle. Christopher (Kit) Marlowe's 1593 play *The Troublesome Reign and Lamentable Death of Edward the Second, King of England, with the Tragical Fall of Proud Mortimer*, usually referred to simply as *Edward II*, describes the reign of King Edward II and his grisly death by having a red hot poker inserted into his bowels, under the orders of Roger Mortimer.

Historians debate whether he did die in this manner, or indeed whether he died in Berkeley Castle. This latter theory is based upon the *Fieschi Letter*, which was sent to his son, King Edward III in 1337 by Manuel Fieschi, an Italian priest who claimed that he escaped from Berkeley and lived as a hermit in the Holy Roman Empire.

Either way, one could argue that the curse of Thomas of Lancaster did come true and some of the events of this tale might have happened.

If you have enjoyed the novel enough to leave a review on **Amazon** and **Goodreads**, then I would be truly grateful. I love to hear from readers, so if you would like to contact me, please do so through my **Facebook** page or send me a message through **Twitter**. You can also see my latest news on my **website**.

Keith Moray

keithmorayauthor.com

Sapere Books is an exciting new publisher of brilliant fiction and popular history.

To find out more about our latest releases and our monthly bargain books visit our website: **saperebooks.com**

Printed in Great Britain
by Amazon